SWALLOWED BY THE COLD

Also by Jensen Beach

For Out of the Heart Proceed

SWALLOWED BY THE COLD

Stories

Jensen Beach

Graywolf Press

The stories in this collection first appeared in the following magazines and journals:
"Animals at Uneasy Rest," in *A Public Space*
"The Drowned Girl," in *American Short Fiction* (online)
"Kino," in *Fifty-Two Stories*
"The Right-Hand Traffic Diversion," in the *Lifted Brow*
"Ships of Stockholm," in *n+1* (online)
"The Apartment," in the *New Yorker*
"Migration," in the *Paris Review*
"The Winter War," in *Sou'wester*
"Henrik Needed Help," in *Spork*
"February 22, 1944," in *Tin House* (online)
"In the Village of Elmsta," in *Witness*

This publication is made possible, in part, by the voters of Minnesota through a Minnesota State Arts Board Operating Support grant, thanks to a legislative appropriation from the arts and cultural heritage fund, and through grants from the National Endowment for the Arts and the Wells Fargo Foundation Minnesota. Significant support has also been provided by Target, the McKnight Foundation, Amazon.com, and other generous contributions from foundations, corporations, and individuals. To these organizations and individuals we offer our heartfelt thanks.

Published by Graywolf Press
250 Third Avenue North, Suite 600
Minneapolis, Minnesota 55401

www.graywolfpress.org

Published in the United States of America

ISBN 978-1-55597-738-2

2 4 6 8 9 7 5 3 1
First Graywolf Printing, 2016

Library of Congress Control Number: 2015953601

Cover design: Kyle G. Hunter

Cover photo: Sheldon Serkin / EyeEM / Getty Images

For Anna
  and
for N, T & E

It is still beautiful to hear the heartbeat
but often the shadow seems more real than the body.

—Tomas Tranströmer (trans. Robert Bly)

Contents

SWALLOWED BY THE COLD

In the Village of Elmsta

In the village of Elmsta, which straddles the mainland and an island about two hours north of Stockholm, there is an uneven asphalt tennis court, veined with cracks and loosely traversed by a shoddy net. It was on this court that Rolf Strand played the best tennis of his life. He lost the first set, but came back to win the next three by an average margin of four games. His opponent—an aging former tennis professional whose prosthetic left arm made a swishing whistle whenever he hit from his backhand—twice broke Rolf's serve, but Rolf was hitting well to both sides and ran the tennis pro to exhaustion. Rolf was happy about this. Who can say how the tennis pro felt? He had only recently lost an arm.

In the canal behind the court, boats waited for a drawbridge to rise. The pilots and passengers of these boats looked up at the bridge impatiently in spite of the nice weather. His summerhouse was on the eastern shore of the island across a small stand of deciduous trees from a family who had twice invited Rolf to dinner and who, he suspected, must have been Buddhists because they were so kind. On his way home from the courts, Rolf rode his bicycle onto the bridge and stopped at its center. He looked at his watch. The leather strap was pliable with sweat. It was twenty minutes of the hour and he felt good. His racket was strapped to the back of his bicycle and did not cause him trouble. He looked down at a sailboat that had come to a stop where the canal narrows to a single lane. Large digital clocks mounted on either side of the bridge notified the boats of the current waiting time. At O'Mally's in Gamla stan, where Rolf had taken a young woman named Karin Johansson on a date nearly fifty years before, a similar clock counted down the minutes remaining until St. Patrick's Day. Karin Johansson died, he remembered reading in the newspaper, in 1988 or 1989.

Facing north, as this sailboat was, he knew it was possible to glimpse, just past the stubby outcropping of rock where the village ends, the open sea. There were nineteen minutes on the clock. If he pedaled hard, he could take the path that ran parallel to the canal out to the Baltic and beat the sailboat to the headland. It would be a simple victory, but still the thought pleased him. It was that kind of day. He hadn't permitted himself to celebrate after his defeat of the former tennis pro and felt somehow cheated by his restraint. His self-control was born out of respect for his opponent's accomplishments, but also the hope that the former tennis pro would agree to a rematch. A second victory might carry him through the two long weeks during which his daughter Matilda and her children would come to visit, as they did every year. These visits caused Rolf significant anxiety about his daily rituals and the various ways his family encroached upon them.

The canal path was rocky and rutted by horse and motorbike use. He considered taking the road instead. That morning he'd placed seven bottles of imported beer in a net, which he strung over the side of his sailing dinghy into the cold water of the inlet across the narrow road from his house. They were by now without a doubt sufficiently chilled. The road would bring him to these beers in the shortest amount of time. But the road was frequently traveled, making it dangerous for bicycles; and, if he decided to take the canal path, he could easily turn due east at its end, walk along a half mile of forest trail, and then bike up a stretch of fire road that ended behind his house. It was a picturesque route. There were sixteen minutes on the clock. He decided to take the path.

The day his second child was born—a boy whom he named Lennart—Rolf walked the canal path in the snow and admired the ice in the canal and the natural beauty of life and barren trees and the storm that had prevented him from driving into Stockholm to witness the birth. He was thinking about this day as he rode the path. The tennis racket shook. He and Lennart had never been close, and he began, as he often did following moments of great pride, to wonder if everything terrible about his life was his own fault. Lennart was back in Stockholm now after five years abroad. He worked for Ericsson first in Morocco then in North Carolina, where Rolf had twice visited. Rolf decided, as he passed a young pine into which someone had carved the crude image of a penis, to call Lennart that afternoon. He planned to grill a fish for his dinner and might, he thought now, give Lennart a call when he was minding the grill with a cold beer in his hand. Lennart's new number was on a notepad by the telephone. Maybe he would invite Lennart to visit the Mamma Andersson exhibit at Moderna Museet.

He tried to refocus his thoughts on his victory over the former tennis pro by listing as best he could remember the former tennis pro's professional achievements. This, he hoped, would bring him back to an appreciation of his victory and away from the regret he felt regarding his son. He thought of the former tennis pro's three consecutive semifinal appearances at the French Open; he remembered the first of these well. Two years into the open era, it was the year his mother, Agneta, died and he'd occupied his grief with an obsessive interest in the Swede's progress in the tournament. He'd spent many afternoons at his summerhouse staring at the light-green wallpaper on the kitchen wall, listening to the matches on the little radio he kept above the sink. There had also been good showings at a tournament in London, and he'd beat Rod Laver in a five-set match in Massachusetts in 1967 that was two minutes short of tying the record for longest championship match in the pre–open era.

Rolf swerved to avoid a deep furrow in the path. The momentum of the bicycle pressed him hard to the right. He leaned to his left. The bicycle wobbled. There was a rock in the middle of the path. He tried to avoid the rock, but the bicycle leaned in the wrong direction and Rolf found himself headed straight for the rock as if he'd been summoned to it. A strum of tension plucked the spokes. He thought he heard himself give a little scream. He flew over the handlebars and landed with a splash in the canal.

The canal was shallow. Rolf struck the bottom with his

head. He tumbled around in the water, grabbing for the surface but touching only the ground. He'd once visited California and could now hear the voice of the lifeguard who taught him to swim in the turbulent Pacific. "Keep calm. Reach slowly for the surface." His toes grazed the rocky bottom. With two paddling sweeps of his arms, he was near enough to the shore to stand. When he did, he felt at once a considerable pain above his left eye. He put his hand to his forehead, and then brought it down to eye level. Watery blood dripped from his fingers. When he flossed his teeth, his gums tended to bleed. He touched his head again and found a large gash about a couple of centimeters above his eyebrow. The wound continued across the ridge of his temple and then turned sharply downward, where it widened to the size of his fist at the sphenoid. He pressed lightly here and, though his fingers were cold and numb, he was sure he felt smooth bone. His eye hurt. "Dammit," he said.

Again he touched the wound and again, bringing his hand down to eye level, he examined the blood on his fingers. The blood was darker. It clung to his fingers like mucus and crept slowly down his arm. His cheek tickled and when he stuck his tongue out, he could taste warm blood collecting in the coarse hair of his mustache, which he had only recently regrown. He began to feel faint. He stepped through the water to the rock-lined shore and climbed up to dry land. There, he removed his shirt and pressed it onto the wound. Then he sat down. Water and blood ran down his face.

The drawbridge rose. He watched this and thought about what to do. He could try to walk back across the bridge. Maybe he would find the tennis pro on the other side. The tennis pro would know what to do. Lacerations to the head can tend to appear more dangerous than they actually are. Even minor wounds might produce a frightening amount of blood. He probably only needed stitches. Rolf was confident in his body's overall conditioning. He'd just defeated a former tennis pro in four sets.

The sailboat, which had now made its way past the drawbridge, motored steadily up the canal toward him. He could hear voices. There was a slight wind, about five knots if he had to guess. He lifted his free hand. "Hello there," he whispered. He didn't mean to whisper, but his throat was beginning to feel constricted and the shout he tried to produce came out in a wet, phlegmy whisper. There were two men and two women all standing in the cockpit. They were tanned and attractive in their shorts and bikinis and sun hats. It was a nice-looking boat, he thought, expensive. He listened to the clean and steady sound of the engine. His left arm felt as though there were an electrical current running through it. He cleared his throat and called out to them again: "Hello there!" The sailboat's pilot appeared to notice that one of the women was pointing at Rolf. The pilot said something to the others. They all looked at Rolf. Rolf waved. He pointed to his bloody T-shirt, then stuck out his pinkie finger and his thumb in what he was sure was the symbol for phone, and held his hand up to his head. The electricity buzzed in his arm and now also in his neck. The passengers waved at him, but the boat didn't slow. He watched the sailboat drift away. On the stern, spelled out in golden letters: *Angelika*. He thought for a moment about this name and the beautiful lettering. He wished he were on board the *Angelika*. It was a perfect day, he thought, as he started to lose consciousness, for sailing. "Don't go," he said. Rolf Strand fell to his side, put his head down on his blood-soaked T-shirt, took one or two shallow breaths, and was dead.

Henrik Brandt tied his sailboat to the mooring ring in the canal. The ring was rusty and drilled into a large stone that stuck out into the canal at such an angle that he'd worried, the first several times he made the trip through the canal, that it would cause an accident. It was one of the first pleasant days of the season. Motorboats, and sailboats, and a handful of kayaks stretched from one side of the narrow canal to the other. For the most part, the people on these boats seemed to enjoy the wait. They laughed and shouted from boat to boat, gossiping about village news. A family from the south of Sweden had recently bought the old Gustafsson place and sold off a dozen acres of the eastern pasture to a developer. The pasture sat up on a small bluff and there were excellent views of the Baltic. It was only a matter of time until the island was overcrowded. Everyone on the canal was convinced of this. Henrik held the rope against the rocking boat. On the mainland side of the canal was the tennis court where the previous summer he'd lost to his wife in three humiliating sets. Even now he felt humiliated. Partly, this was because he liked playing tennis and had, the afternoon his wife beat him so resolutely, made such an ordeal of the loss that he hadn't played again out of embarrassment, and partly because it shamed him to remember how dreadfully he'd acted. It was a game. He lost. There was nothing wrong with losing at tennis to your own wife. But still he hadn't played in over a year. Slowly, he'd grown accustomed to this and had turned his attention to other activities. That summer, he and Lisa had

taken their bikes out almost daily and ridden to the fisherman and back in the early morning fog. He'd been sailing
the boat more frequently than in previous summers and had
once or twice considered taking up kayaking. Henrik hadn't
let himself watch the French Open that year, and he hadn't
once glanced at the supplement in *Dagens Nyheter* about the
Swedish Davis Cup team. Tennis was eroding from his life.

Much had changed for Henrik recently. Within the last
five years, he'd left his job at Nordea Bank and taken a new
position at a law firm, which tripled his salary and allowed
him to buy a summerhouse on the eastern shore of the island,
a few miles from the village. When he bought the house, he
had a dock built, at the end of which he kept his sailboat, the
Angelika—so named for his oldest sister, who'd died from leukemia when Henrik was six. On the day that the marina determined every fall, Henrik sailed his boat south to Norrtälje
and paid the crane operator to lift the *Angelika* into dry storage. He enjoyed sailing, although he wasn't particularly good
at it. Since the previous September, Henrik had been sleeping
with a colleague's wife. This colleague's name was Peter, and
Henrik had invited him and his wife, Helle, out for a week at
the house. He and Peter were not especially close at work, but
he wanted to see Helle. It was the last week of June and soon
the whole country would be on vacation. He thought they
might sail to Finland if conditions were good.

Peter and Helle arrived on Friday and the four of them
spent the weekend walking the trails on the interior of the
island, waiting out the weather. Henrik was an inexperienced
sailor and it was windy.

During the Cold War, the military built a series of bun-
kers along the water on the island's eastern shoreline, all of

which were now abandoned and derelict. Henrik and Peter spent much of Monday afternoon trying to pry open the thick metal door of the bunker nearest the house. They were mindful of snakes. The wind blew salty air at their faces, carried to their ears the arguments of the birds out on the thin tombolo, which connects the island to a large rock Henrik had been told was called Bull's Head. Henrik cut his hand on a jagged piece of metal that was obscured by a patch of thick brush. The wound was deep and bled profusely. He didn't believe he needed stitches and his tetanus was up to date, so when he and Peter returned to the house, Henrik asked Lisa to clean and dress the wound but he disagreed with her suggestion to drive to the clinic in town.

The following day, Tuesday, the wind calmed. They left at ten, taking with them a picnic of sandwiches and freshly boiled new potatoes, which they ate cold with sour cream. By the early afternoon they'd made it to the southern entrance of the canal. Henrik chose to go north up the canal to get back to the house rather than backtrack around the island's southern tip. He was eager to motor for a stretch, draw in the sails, uncomplicate his day. Elmsta was pretty from the water. They were unlucky with the drawbridge.

He watched the clock count down the minutes until the drawbridge rose. The cut on his hand stung and he concentrated on this. Lisa had helped him rebandage his hand that morning. A man on a bicycle stopped on the bridge, peering down at them. Henrik couldn't see the man well enough in the bright sun to recognize him but the stark shadow of his posture up there on the bridge struck Henrik as familiar and a little bit sad. There were dozens of sad old men on the island. It could have been any of them. Before he was able to get caught thinking endlessly about it, he was distracted by his wife and Helle. Helle and Lisa were talking about a movie they'd both recently seen. The movie had made them both cry and they were sharing this, eagerly admitting to tears. On the mainland side of the canal, near the concrete pylons, Henrik watched a man fish. The gossip between the other boats had quieted, and many people sat with their feet in the water, impatiently splashing. After a quarter of an hour, the traffic signals on the island and the mainland flashed red and the large gears beneath the arms of the bridge became visible, articulating upward. A bell sounded. Henrik let the bridge reach at least sixty degrees before he passed beneath it. It seemed only reasonable.

Not far after the bridge, Helle waved to someone on the shore. There was a bicycle lying on its side and a man sat beside it with something, a T-shirt, Henrik thought, held up to his head. He was sure this was Jesper, the village drunk who, he didn't know, had died that spring. Jesper was struck by lightning while searching for Viking relics in an abandoned pasture on the island's northwest corner. "It's Jesper," Henrik said and waved. "He's fallen from his bike." They all turned to look at the accident and the man waved to them and made some kind of gesture toward his head. Helle raised her arm to wave again at the man and Henrik looked at her right breast. As they passed, Henrik thought he heard Jesper call out to them. He turned to the noise, but was careful to keep one hand steady on the wheel. The canal was shallow at its edges. The man fell to his side. Several hundred yards inland, the spot where Jesper's body had been discovered was still marked by orange flagging tape that no one had bothered to remove. It flapped in the wind and no one saw it.

The Baltic was open in front of them. On cold days, cargo ships passed upside down on the horizon. Henrik spent hours in the early fall searching for these mirages through a pair of old binoculars he found when he and Lisa moved their summer things into the house. He rounded the headland smoothly. The wind was blowing a little harder across the open water and he could have let out the sails, had some fun. Instead, he tucked in close to the coastline, giving it just enough throttle to keep the boat at a comfortable speed.

Docking made him nervous, but he guided the boat in easily. Peter and Helle dropped the fenders over the side, and the boat nudged the dock. Lisa jumped to the dock and tied up the boat with two knots. Henrik cut the engine and began preparations. This was his favorite part of owning a boat: securing lines, covering sails, wiping up shoeprints and water from the deck. Lisa wanted to go back to the house immediately. It was midafternoon and she'd planned a marinade for the pork. Peter followed her; he needed to make a phone call. This left Helle and Henrik alone, together, on the boat. Henrik watched his wife and colleague walk up the path to the house. A low slope of red rock jutted into the path. Peter walked up onto it and then jumped down, as a child might. The sun was shining.

Henrik wiped down the cockpit with a damp towel in his good hand. He worked more slowly than he normally did, enjoying Helle's concentration on him. He admired his own forearm. It was tan and muscular. Helle put her hand on top of Henrik's. "I've missed you," she said. He took her hand and led her down the steep ladder into the cabin, where they made love quickly, leaning against the door of the head. When he was finished, Henrik tucked his still-erect penis back into his shorts. They walked slowly up the path to the house. He avoided the red rock.

Inside, Peter was sitting on the couch, reading a biography of Abraham Lincoln in English. Lisa was in the kitchen. There was the sound of the coffeepot finishing and the smell of the previous night's pie warming in the oven. They drank coffee and ate pie and laughed. The rest of the afternoon passed this way, and soon Henrik found himself on the back deck with a glass of scotch in front of a newly flaming barbeque. Peter was leaning against the deck railing next to the barbeque. The tomato plant Henrik planted that spring was coming along nicely. Peter had, for the last several minutes, been talking his way around a delicate work issue for which Henrik was indirectly responsible. Henrik nodded and agreed and promised, as he'd done twice previously, to look into the issue on Peter's behalf. It pained him to lie; there was nothing he could do about the problem. Henrik hoped that without his saying so Peter understood this and was after reassurance rather than action. Their wives came out onto the deck. Lisa set a plate full of vegetable skewers down on the small table beside the barbeque. Helle held two glasses of white wine, one of which she handed to Lisa. A smoking citronella candle on the deck produced a silky cloud of smoke from behind the table. Peter made an awkward toast to another good day with good friends. Henrik and Helle looked at each other. Clouds were moving in over the Baltic. He suspected rain by sunset.

After the table was set and the four of them sat down in the places Lisa had assigned them and the wine was poured and the meat cut, the telephone rang. Henrik got up to answer. The phone at the summerhouse didn't often ring, so he immediately suspected the worst, although he had no guess as to what the worst might be.

He took three long steps across the kitchen and answered the phone on the third ring. It was Fredrik Holm, chairman of the homeowners' association, with whom Henrik had had a bitter argument the previous winter regarding the dues he and Lisa were expected to pay for snowplowing. "I'm calling with bad news," Fredrik Holm said. "Rolf Strand passed away earlier today. He appears to have had a bicycle accident. A young girl, the Källström girl, found him this afternoon."

Rolf lived three houses down, and Henrik had often run into him out walking in the evenings. "I'm sorry to hear it," he said.

Fredrik explained that the accident had occurred at around one in the afternoon, just after he and Rolf had finished their tennis match. "Rolf was on his way home," Fredrik said. "For some reason he took the canal path. I can't imagine why."

Before he could stop himself, Henrik said, "I saw a man on the canal path this afternoon. We were out with the boat." He immediately regretted admitting this. The inconvenience of now having placed himself, however circumstantially, into the event bore down on the rest of his evening. He dreaded further explaining the afternoon to Fredrik and was eager to get back to the meal. Before the phone rang, Helle had, when she sat down beside him, hooked her foot around his leg and begun stroking it up and down. Even as he listened to Fredrik go on and on about neighborliness and immutable responsibilities, Henrik felt aroused. After a late fall and winter during which Henrik and Helle had only seen each other sporadically, he'd lately found himself eager to spend more time with her.

There was a great deal of blood on the canal path that afternoon, Fredrik insisted. It was a gruesome scene. Henrik tried to concentrate on this, but Helle's thighs were so smooth and round. He heard her voice out on the back deck. She was laughing. Her bikini bottom had stretched across her hips in such a way that he had earlier wondered if he didn't want to have children someday after all. There's something uncontrollable inside of me, he thought.

"Why didn't you stop?" Fredrik asked him.

He pictured Rolf Strand lying facedown on the dusty canal path, thick tributaries of blood surrounding the body. He turned and looked out the small kitchen window to the deck. Helle waved at him, and he loved her, he was sure of it. He took a deep breath. "I saw a man sitting on the canal path," he said, somewhat defiant now. "Who's to say it was even Rolf?" He picked at a dried splash of something brown on the counter with his thumbnail. His buzz was slipping away and he felt cold in his shoulders. "Whoever it was we saw seemed to be fine. He waved at us."

"I would have stopped," Fredrik said.

Outside, he took his seat, and sighed deeply. Lisa was just placing her knife and fork across her empty plate. He'd always found comfort in the thoughtless, habitual actions. "What is it?" she asked.

"Rolf Strand died," he said.

"The grumpy old man from down the road? That's terrible."

Henrik took a bite of his cold meat, sipped his wine. "It was a bicycle accident."

"My god," Helle said.

"It happened early this afternoon. On the canal path. We may have seen it. I told him we didn't see anything. We would have stopped if we'd seen anything."

"Told who, Henrik? Who was on the phone?" Lisa asked. "Henrik?"

"Fredrik Holm," he said.

"The tennis player?" asked Lisa.

Henrik pushed his silverware across his plate loudly, and refilled his glass. "Yes," he said.

"Lisa," Helle said, "is that the man with one arm? The tennis player with only one arm?" They both laughed and then Peter joined in, laughing and saying, "You never told me about him, you never told me about him!" at Helle repeatedly, as though he were happy to have missed out on the joke. And Lisa, tucking a strand of her blond hair behind her ear, said, "You're terrible! Someone's died. He's dead. We shouldn't laugh," she said, laughing. Henrik remembered an article that had appeared recently in *DN*. A boy last winter had been beaten to death outside a club in Stockholm while a line of people waiting to get inside watched and did nothing. It was a different country than it used to be.

"What a terrible accident," Lisa said, composing herself now, but still amused. She was clearing her throat and crossing and uncrossing her legs. Henrik was sure he saw Helle bite her lip and stifle a smile.

"I'm glad we didn't see anything," Helle said. "I'm happy we didn't stop. I can't stomach blood."

"Neither can Henrik," Lisa said. "You should have seen how he squirmed when I was bandaging his hand." Peter laughed at this and Helle smiled at Henrik. He felt his hand very distinctly.

Later, after the dishes had been washed, and Lisa had put on a fresh pot of coffee, and Henrik had gone to his study for a bottle of brandy, it was quiet. Henrik sat on the couch facing the large bay window in the living room and watched the heavy rain boil the sea in the late-night dusk. He knew, of course, that by dwelling on the day's coincidence, as awful as it may have been, he was being unfair to himself and to Lisa and to their guests. His mood had turned sour shortly after dinner and he hadn't spoken more than half a sentence to Peter, who'd tried to engage Henrik earlier but now sat in front of the fireplace and tossed paper napkins into the flames. Henrik sipped his drink and took deep breaths and tried to enjoy the warmth of the house. But even Helle, her perfect body, the softness of her breasts in the thin sweater she'd put on when the rain started, appeared to him dirtied by Rolf Strand.

Lisa and Helle eventually found their way to the couch, where they sat close to each other and continued a conversation they'd been having about books. It disturbed Henrik, as he watched the two women, to see that Helle was able to feign such innocence. There she was, whispering animatedly about a novel she'd recently enjoyed and Lisa was nodding her head and saying that, yes, she'd enjoyed those very same qualities, and they were laughing. Henrik thought about the way Helle had that afternoon turned her head back toward him and whispered her approval as he entered her, and he felt something like rage building in his chest. Helle reached out and touched Lisa's wrist with her fingertips and they both laughed again.

Henrik stood up and cleared his throat. "A man died today," he said.

"Henrik, please," Lisa said.

"A man died today," he said, ignoring his wife. "We did nothing about it. We had the chance and we did nothing."

"It was an awful coincidence," said Peter, who stood up and put a hand on Henrik's shoulder. "Don't let it get to you." Even at the office, Peter was eager to move on from whatever conflict might have been dragging on the day.

"We had no way of knowing," Helle said.

Henrik concentrated on the warm reflection of the fireplace in the window. Before Rolf, he'd once seen a dead body covered by a thick gray blanket in the street next to the scene of a car accident. It was snowing then and there was blood in the snow and paramedics lingering about the body. An arm had slipped out from under the blanket and by the rings on the fingers Henrik could tell the body had belonged to a woman. Outside, the rain fell hard against the gutters. "Helle and I are sleeping together," he said quietly.

"Henrik," Lisa said.

"I told her I loved her, but I don't think it's true," he said, turning now to face his wife.

Lisa got up from the couch and looked at Helle. "What's he saying?"

"Henrik," said Helle.

"I want to live in a place where someone will stop and help me if I'm dying on a dirt path." He cleared his throat again as if he were going to speak further on the subject but did not.

"You're drunk," Lisa said. "You're only drunk."

"Probably," he said. He sat back down and picked up his glass. "Probably," he said, and took a drink.

Peter walked to the window and then back to the fire-place, where he sat down on the hearth and said, "I'm uncomfortable with all this." Helle, who'd moved to one end of the couch, crossed and uncrossed her legs and pulled at the neck of her sweater. Lisa poured herself another drink from the bottle on the coffee table. During his military service, Henrik was stationed in Boden, where during the daylight of summer nights he often lay awake and worried about Lisa. He was sure she'd been playing a cruel joke when she told him she loved him in a letter. She was still at Uppsala then, studying psychology, and Henrik had at first thought she was conducting some kind of psychological experiment on him. It was a fragile time. He twice masturbated to the thought of one of his fellow soldiers. That autumn, he participated in a survival course taught by a middle-aged South African army officer who spoke terrible Swedish and once slapped Henrik over a misunderstanding. Henrik was taught a neck hold with which it was possible to make someone unconscious. He considered doing this if Peter were to try anything. He was trying to remember the second step of the neck hold when Helle suddenly stood up, straightened her sweater, and said, "That's about it for me." She then sat back down and looked at Peter. Henrik remembered the proper position for his arms and felt his shoulders move slightly as he visualized the movements. "You think this is funny?" Lisa asked him.

"I don't know what it's supposed to be," said Henrik.

"The day started so well," Peter said. He got up from the hearth, emptied his glass in a single gulp, and left the room. Helle followed not long after, and Henrik and Lisa sat in silence, listening to the restrained yelling in the guest room. Henrik listened for his name. This lasted until Lisa flinched as if she were completing some motion she began long ago. She stood in front of Henrik and was looking at him but, it seemed to Henrik, not really *looking* at him until she swallowed twice and then turned and walked away. She stumbled on the step between the living room and the hall and said, "Fuck you, Henrik," into the darkness in front of her.

There was nothing to do but go.

Outside, the rain had stopped and the sky was clearing from the horizon inward, clouds peeling back across the rocky landscape. The water in the shallow inlet opposite the house gurgled. Rainwater ran down the driveway. Rolf's sailing dinghy drummed hollowly off a smooth rock in the inlet. The net with Rolf's beer was still attached, and would remain so until his son came in the late fall to take the boat out of the water for the winter. Henrik stood in the driveway and rested his bandaged hand on the wet roof of his car. The wind was blowing and thick drops of rainwater fell from the shaking trees all around him. He checked his watch. It was half past two. Already there was a wash of pink and orange on the horizon and the dark silhouette of a single, stubborn cloud.

Because he couldn't think of what else to do, Henrik circled his house in the dark. The light in the guest room was still on, its long rectangle of light falling on the deck. He watched Helle and Peter's shadows pass in and out of this rectangle. He thought he'd probably never been so intensely discussed. Several of his tomatoes were ripe. He made his way around the house and peered into his own bedroom window, curious to see how his wife might be responding to all this. She was in bed and appeared to be asleep.

At the bunker, he checked the entrance in case he and Peter had somehow succeeded in unlocking the door without knowing it. The door was still tightly locked. His hand ached as if it were aware of being close to where he'd injured it.

He was careful on the slippery rocks. From the point of Bull's Head, Henrik watched the horizon, but soon became bored and tired. The wind was blowing and the sea was loud. He was very tired. And he had to pee. The sun would rise soon and with it the noisy gulls and the fisherman from down around the point who took his old motorboat up every morning to check the fyke nets fastened to Bull's Head. The eel population in the Baltic was diminishing, but still every year the fisherman set his nets. Helle and Peter were no doubt leaving that morning and Henrik couldn't go home until that had happened. He would try to set things right with Lisa, possibly salvage some of the remaining two weeks of his vacation. Until then, he thought, as he urinated into the frothy Baltic, it was best to stay away.

He kneeled on the darkened porch, his bandaged hand stuck elbow-deep into a black opening underneath the top step, and reached for the spare key. Rolf had once told him it was there. The dirt was wet and he moved his fingers through it slowly, searching for the key.

It was cold inside Rolf Strand's house. Henrik removed a thick wool sweater from a hook by the door and wrapped it around his shoulders. He poured himself a drink and looked around the house. It was larger than his house, but more crowded with furniture. There was a picture window on the eastern wall through which he planned to watch the sunrise.

There were dirty dishes in the sink, and the shell of an egg arranged neatly in a small pile on a plate on the table. *Svenska Dagbladet* was open to the sports section beside the plate. This permanence of things whose nature was temporary renewed his sadness, so he began tidying up. He placed the rest of the dishes in the sink and folded and placed the paper on top of the pile beside the fireplace. He swept a dried footprint out of the back door and straightened the pillows on the couch. He opened the door to each of the rooms and looked inside. There was a musty smell in many of them. He discovered a home office, and an exercise room in which an elliptical machine was positioned in front of a large television. In the back of the house, there was a bedroom with a small bed covered neatly by a floral bedspread. He checked in the closet. He tore clothes off their hangers, pulled boxes of photographs down from a shelf. He rifled through books from the bookcase in the living room, and got down on his hands and knees to inspect the far corners of a floor cabinet. He was looking for proof, he supposed, that Rolf deserved it.

In the kitchen, he poured another drink. Under the couch cushions, he found what amounted to nearly one hundred kronor in small coins. He left the cushions on the floor. There was a pornographic magazine in the magazine rack in the downstairs bathroom. It was French. Henrik thumbed through it but was not aroused. He returned to the kitchen and pulled one of the stools up to the counter. From this position it was possible for him to glimpse a small corner of his own driveway. Peter and Helle's car was still parked beneath the narrow birch that later in the summer would partly obscure the front window of his house. He planned to sit and wait until the car was gone and then go home to his wife. There was nothing else to do. Whatever he had had with Helle was over, no question. She must have made this decision by now. His hand was bleeding and blood had seeped through the bandage. He ripped a paper towel from the roll beside the sink and stuffed it inside the bandage to absorb the blood. On the counter was the notepad on which Rolf had written Lennart's telephone number. Henrik decided to call this number, and when a voice answered, he hesitated for only a moment.

Kino

From across the room Martin was trying to monitor his wife. They were at a fiftieth birthday party for Louise's friend Pernilla, and it was getting late. He'd planned on taking Louise home before she could drink too much. But for the past hour he'd been talking with Pernilla's son, whom he recognized from the Kino Club in Stockholm, and had lost track of Louise. Oskar made change for the video booths at the Kino Club. He was a nervous boy with long fingers that never stopped moving from his face to a button on his green shirt and back to his face. For several minutes, he'd been talking about the variety of modern coffin-building materials. He was standing very close to Martin, close enough to lean into him, which he did whenever he laughed. Martin watched Louise disappear into the kitchen empty-handed and later reappear in the living room with a fresh drink. She careened from conversation to conversation. Oskar kept talking. Martin was sure Oskar recognized him. Louise laughed loudly. She danced alone to the music. Oskar smelled good. He'd just finished a course at Uppsala, he told Martin, on the history of burial practices. "I'm mostly interested in the environmental impacts," he said, leaning close to Martin and only catching himself with a pinch of his fingers on Martin's sleeve. "Do you know they can make diamonds from the carbon of a cremated corpse?"

Louise staggered toward them from across the room. She was beginning to show signs. Her left eyelid drooped as if part of her brain were shutting down. Martin heard Oskar say, "Banana leaf eco-coffin," and saw Louise's eye begin to twitch and her head cock to the right. She was prone to compromised vision. Martin excused himself, took Louise by the elbow, and led her from the room.

Louise struggled to keep up. She said "excuse us, excuse us" as they walked down the empty hall. "Martin," Louise said, "I was enjoying myself."

"So was I," he said.

Outside, the rain had cleared and the sky was pale. They walked slowly toward the car. Martin felt Louise's weight against him. "Anyway," she said, "it's all very tragic, apparently. Totally heartbreaking." She lost her balance, stumbled slightly. Martin had to hold her by the elbow to keep her standing. "These shoes," she said.

"What's heartbreaking, Louise?" Martin asked.

"Pernilla's son was nearly finished with his boat when someone set fire to the whole marina," Louise said and added, "for insurance money, Pernilla suspects."

Martin had once owned a boat. It was a small catamaran,

the sort of boat it was possible to launch from a beach. He enjoyed sailing the catamaran although it was light and unwieldy in the wind. When he and Louise married, he donated the boat to the sailing club in Årstaviken, where he'd taken lessons as a boy. "Did they salvage it?" he asked. They were far enough from the house that they couldn't hear the hum of conversation or music from the open windows. The air was cool and the wind blew gently from the west. Martin felt it on his neck. It was July. He thought briefly of Oskar and what he might say to him the next time he saw him at the Kino Club.

"I didn't catch the whole story," Louise said. "But I guess Oskar, that's the son's name, had been working on the boat for two years. He was planning to sail it to Peru. Can you imagine?"

"There's a lot of ocean between here and Peru," Martin said. He pictured Oskar under the hot equatorial sun, the vast glassy expanse of the Atlantic spread out around him, veins of salty sweat dripping down his face and body.

"That's where Oskar comes from," Louise said. "He's adopted."

"He was telling me about his studies. Did you know they've invented biodegradable coffins?"

"I don't know what that means," Louise said. "Oskar has contacted his birth mother. He did it behind Pernilla's back. She's very upset. I just try to imagine how hurt I would be." She stopped to remove her shoes, balancing herself with a hand on Martin's shoulder. He concentrated on providing resistance. Louise lifted her foot and reached to take off her shoe. She then turned around and repeated the process with the other hand and other foot. He looked ahead and Louise looked back toward the house. She held one of her shoes against Martin's shoulder. He smelled sweat and leather.

"I wonder if we left something," Louise said. Oskar's steps made thin, sharp grinding noises on the asphalt. She had a shoe in each hand and lifted them up in front of her at Oskar. "You're not supposed to appear out of nowhere like that. How funny."

Oskar scratched his arm. The veins in his hands were visible even in the twilight. "Are these yours?" he asked. He lifted a brown purse straight out in front of him.

"That's only one thing," Louise said.

Oskar dropped the purse to his side. It dangled from its strap, grazed his knee. "Can you drive me someplace?" he asked.

Martin looked at his watch. "It's late," he said.

"I'm waiting for a call. I'm meeting a friend but I don't know where. Is the city center on your way? I'm meeting a friend there but I don't know where yet." He laughed. "That's funny, I don't know where I'm going only that I have to go there." It had been clear to Martin that Oskar was drunk, or nearly so, at the party, but now it was obvious.

Louise insisted Oskar ride in the front. They hadn't been on the road very long when Louise said she felt unwell. "I'm going to close my eyes," she said. "Just for a moment."

Martin rolled the window down. "Whose purse is that?" he asked.

"I found it," said Oskar.

"You shouldn't take things," Martin said. He heard Oskar shift in his seat, and felt the weight and warmth of Oskar's hand on his thigh. He looked down to see if he'd only imagined it. "Oskar," he said quietly, "what are you doing?"

"You think you're keeping it a secret," Oskar said. He was smiling widely. "But you're not."

"You've mistaken me for someone else."

"I've made change for you," said Oskar. "Booth 16. That's your favorite."

Martin closed his eyes. "Whose purse is it, Oskar?"

"What's your wife's name again?"

"Louise," said Martin.

"I think I remember seeing the purse," Louise said suddenly from the backseat. "At the party. I saw the purse at the party, but I can't remember who was holding it." In the rearview mirror, Louise's eyes were closed tight.

Oskar squeezed Martin's thigh once and then took his hand away, sitting up straight and energetically. He reached into the purse, took out a piece of paper. "Let's see," he said in a loud, clear voice. "A list. Bank, metro pass, rent." Oskar turned around to look at Louise in the backseat. "Other people's lives are so boring." Martin noticed the skin stretched taut across Oskar's throat. He wanted to reach out and touch it.

The tires whispered loudly outside on the wet street. In the distance, red and white beams of light dashed up and down the freeway. "Slow down, Martin," Louise said. "I'm beginning to feel dizzy."

Oskar turned back around in his seat. He put his hand back on Martin's thigh. Martin felt each finger move closer to his crotch. He put his own hand on top of Oskar's as if to confirm that it was really there.

"I'm right, aren't I? Booth 16?"

"That side of the club is quiet," Martin said.

"I'm a very spiritual person," Oskar said. "It's part of my heritage."

Martin pushed himself forward in his seat, pressed his right leg against Oskar's palm.

"I recognized this immediately," said Oskar.

Martin closed his eyes again. The traffic light at the intersection turned yellow and then red as Martin passed beneath it. There was a long, high note from an approaching horn. He swerved to avoid the side of a speeding van. The car overtook the curb and jounced onto the sidewalk. It came off a narrow stretch of grass with a jolt into an empty supermarket parking lot. They weren't far from the street. Martin heard the steady honk of a horn behind him but was too scared to turn around to see if he'd caused an accident.

"Stop honking the horn," Louise said.

At the sound of his wife's voice, Martin flinched and looked at his lap to see if Oskar's hand was still there.

"I think I'm bleeding," Oskar said. He opened his door and spit a mouthful of blood to the asphalt. "I must have bit my lip," he said. He got out of the car and doubled over, leaning on the open door. "I swallowed blood. I don't feel well." He made a sharp retching noise, doubled over, and vomited. Martin heard it slap to the ground.

"Martin," Louise shrieked, "he got sick."

Martin didn't say anything.

Oskar coughed and heaved twice more and collapsed back into the car, pulling his legs in after him. He breathed heavily. Martin watched his chest move. "In the fall," Oskar said after a long time, "I'm traveling to Peru. I've always wanted to see Machu Picchu. It's part of my heritage. Do you know I'm adopted? Has Pernilla told you?"

"Your mother told me about your boat," Louise said. She

put her hand on Oskar's head. "Do you feel better?" Her fingers were obscured beneath the curls.

Martin reached out and touched Oskar's cheek with his fingertips. "What's our destination?" he asked.

"Please, Martin," Louise said, brushing Martin's hand away. "Try to be sensitive."

Oskar wiped his mouth with the back of his hand. "It's all right. I feel much better now," he said.

The purse was in Oskar's lap. His hands lay tenderly over it. No one said anything. Oskar closed his eyes, breathed deeply. Louise kept her hand on Oskar's head. After a little while she stopped stroking his hair, but she didn't remove her hand.

"Lima is located inside a basin," Oskar said finally. His eyes were still closed. "I've only ever seen pictures. I have family there. They're going to let me stay with them when I arrive. Of course, I haven't asked them yet, but I'm sure they will," he said. "I'm sure they will."

"It sounds like a beautiful city," said Louise.

"I've always wanted to see where I come from," Oskar said. He wiped his mouth with his hand again. Martin watched the tall birch on the edge of the parking lot shudder with the wind. It was all gone. Under the car's interior light Oskar's face appeared yellow and sickly.

"Look," Martin said, "I'm sorry. I was distracted. It's late, and I'm tired."

"It took me three tries to get my boat to catch. First I tried to light a seat cushion."

"Excuse me?" Louise said.

Oskar stepped out of the car. He adjusted the purse over

his shoulder. Martin couldn't see his face. "I used diesel fuel," Oskar said. "That's how I got the boat to light. Diesel fuel and towels. It was much harder than I expected. The seats just melted. There must have been some kind of retardant on them."

"Oskar," said Louise, "you shouldn't lie about serious things."

"I've heard a lot of the other boats are damaged. No one will believe me, of course, but I only wanted to destroy my own boat. I hated it."

"You set it on fire?" Martin said. "Is that what you're saying?"

"He's only drunk," Louise said.

"I did," said Oskar. He took a step away from the car.

Louise said something unintelligible. Martin watched her lift herself from the seat and drop back down again. "What's wrong with you?" he asked.

Oskar leaned forward so that his body stretched into the car up to his shoulders. "I'm not afraid anymore," he said. "You shouldn't be so scared of yourself."

"What does that mean?" asked Louise.

Martin turned the ignition fully off and removed the key. The interior light went out. Oskar walked away from the car and back toward the street. In the mirror, Martin watched Oskar approach the dim circle of red light from the traffic signal at the intersection. Before Oskar reached the light, he turned around. The purse hung from his shoulder.

"Come on," Martin said, spitting the words out to himself. He got out of the car and walked toward Oskar. "I'll take you home," he said loudly. It was lighter now than it had been when they left the party. He heard Louise get out of the car, close the door.

"I'm tired," she said.

The traffic lights changed and the washes of green and red on the asphalt switched places. "We'll take you home, Oskar," Martin said. "You don't feel well."

A car passed, going in the direction they'd come. Oskar crossed to the middle of the street. Another car approached, this time coming from the opposite direction, and Oskar jogged the rest of the way across. At the other side of the street he turned and looked back at Martin and Louise.

"Just let him go," Louise said. "Please. We have a long drive home."

Martin stepped out into the street and crossed to the center divide. He stood between lanes, waiting for a car, approaching quickly from the right, to pass.

February 22, 1944

He felt the sound before he heard it. It was late, probably too late for boats to come into the bay from the lake. The sluice gates did sometimes freeze in winter. Perhaps he had heard the motor of the gate straining against the ice down in the narrow bay just to the south. Or else he had heard a truck or a bus slipping on an icy patch on the bridge, engines revved too high. But as the sound got louder, grew from a deep rumble to a more distinct hum, out of his body and to his ear, it took shape and he was able to picture the planes above. He could not be sure how many but there were several. For four years, Bent had been waiting for the war to arrive. He had watched it spread and smolder on the continent and through the Pacific. Photographs and newsreels every day depicted new horrors. The fighting had intensified in Finland in recent weeks. Early February, the Soviets and the Finnish had signed an armistice but the bombings on Helsinki had not stopped. They had intensified, obviously designed to force a Finnish surrender. He knew this was not a good sign that Sweden could stay neutral. The war had finally come. It was right above him. Yet, beyond the orange glow of the street-lamps he saw only stars in a clear sky, not the earthy shapes of low-flying planes he expected. He took a step into the street, checked to his right for oncoming traffic, and, seeing that there was none, began to cross.

It was a quarter after eight in the evening. A storm had earlier cleared and there was a layer of fresh snow on the ground. He was on his way home from an evening out with Agneta, a woman he knew from Karolinska Institute, where he was studying to become a pediatrician. She worked in one of the libraries. They had had tea and talked about the Continuation War. Tensions had not resolved following the Winter War in 1940 and by 1941, the Continuation War had broken out, consuming the Karelian Isthmus. The Continuation War was on everyone's mind. Swedish newspapers reported casualties daily. The bombings were targeted farther and farther west, first Åbo, then Åland. Stockholm could be next. Bent feared that one way or the other this new war would spill across the Baltic, drag Sweden the way of Norway and Denmark. For three months in 1940, he had fought in Finland. His volunteer unit was assigned to a position near the line at Märkäjärvi. The fighting had shaken him, driven him strongly into support for a neutral Sweden. Even four years later, his attempts to forget were too easily peeled back to reveal images of icy blood and searing wounds from mortar shrapnel. He had never before and not since felt a cold like that winter. The branches of the pines were so heavy with snow they sagged lower than his head. The earth in the trenches was frozen solid and every morning new bruises appeared on his legs from crouching in the dirt.

The sound grew still louder. It was a wave pounding down on the city, impossibly close. He neared the other side of the street. A car was approaching from his left, so he took two short, quick steps toward the curb. A young woman on the sidewalk looked up at him just as he stepped onto the curb. Her hair was darker and her hips broader, yet she reminded him of Agneta. He was eager to see Agneta again. They had plans to meet the following day. The thought made him smile. Just as he did, he was struck in the face by the hail of an erupting window. He fell to his right side and could not hear. Snow soaked through his pants, clung to his coat and hair. Shoes rushed toward him and away from him. Faintly past the blur of feet and legs he saw soldiers, white-capped, rifles drawn. He heard orders shouted into the thin cold air, steam billowing from open mouths. The round, aching pain in his shoulder brought him back to the pavement. He knew at once he had broken bones. This was a diagnosis he had no trouble making. He opened his eyes and saw that a man stood over him. The man shouted, "The blast knocked you over, the blast knocked you over."

The pain in his shoulder made it difficult to see. He knew of no physiological reason for this but it was true. The young woman who had reminded him of Agneta stumbled back in his direction. She held her hands to her face. From between her fingers, blood dripped down the backs of her hands and over her wrists. He called out to her, not knowing what had happened, only that she needed help and that his shoulder hurt. The pain radiated outward in a dull circumference. His coat was soaked through with snow. He tried to stand. The woman kept her hands to her face. She backed up slowly to the corner of the building and leaned against the quoining. Her shoulders were even with one of the horizontal intersections. She began to slide downward into a sitting position. Her dress caught on the building's facade and rode gently upward over her knees. Through his pain, he was aware of the tops of her stockings and the whiteness of her thighs. She dropped her hands to her side to brace against the sidewalk, and she sat. Blood pulsed from two deep lacerations to the right side of her face, one directly below her eye and the other stretching the length of her jaw. He looked for help but found only empty streets and smoke and flames rising from behind the trees at the edge of the park. He was in a Stockholm he no longer recognized, and he understood at once that here anything at all might reasonably transpire.

Anniversary

She was running up a gentle rise in the path toward him. Henrik worked with her husband, Peter, and had met her several times, so he recognized her immediately. When they'd passed each other, he slowed down and turned, sensing she'd done the same. It was unusual for him to stop his run to talk with someone he knew, even if he knew that person well, but the morning had been pleasant and he was in a good mood in spite of the approaching clouds, and she'd smiled at him in such a way that he thought he should stop to say hello. They each waved, Henrik walking back up the hill and Helle down it.

"You're out running," he said when he felt he was close enough for her to hear him.

"I am," she said. "You too."

"I didn't know you ran," he said. He rested one of his feet on a root near the edge of the path.

She laughed. There was a teasing lilt to her laugh and he felt at once close to her. "No," she said. "How could you?"

He breathed in the thick, musty smell of sweat and didn't know if it was hers or his. "You know runners. I'm surprised you've never tried to compare kilometer pace with me." He smiled at her to indicate he was teasing her back.

"I'm not that kind of runner," she said. "Not yet anyhow. I've only just started in the spring."

"I haven't been running long either," he said. This was a lie. He'd been running seriously since his military service. At first he ran to maintain his weight, but it'd long been a compulsion, a part of his life he couldn't imagine giving up. On average he broke thirty kilometers a week. It made him nervous to try to predict when and in what situations he might need to uphold a lie, and he found himself, without a sense that he could control this action, digging the toe of his running shoe into the dirt in front of him as if he were drawing a line he was daring himself to cross. "It's something I picked up about a year ago," he said.

Helle rocked from side to side, shifting her weight from one leg to the other. "Do you often run in the park?" she asked.

"Three times a week in good weather," he said.

"You must live close to here," she said. "I don't think I know where you live."

"Not far. In Vasastan."

"I had two hours between meetings this afternoon so I decided to take advantage of the sun." She indicated toward the sky with her hand. After a clear morning, clouds were already moving in over the city again. It'd been a stormy summer. "We live in Enskede," she said. A breeze came rustling through the woods beside the path, carrying with it the first leaves of fall and, inexplicably, the smell of a public swimming pool—strongly chlorinated yet mildewed air—a smell that triggered arousal in Henrik. He'd always assumed this arousal had something to do with the summer he and Edvin Forsberg discovered it was possible to see inside the women's locker room at the Blackeberg Swimming Hall from directly to the right of the water fountain opposite the locker room entrance. "We've been there for five years," Helle said.

"Where's that?" asked Henrik. He felt himself being pulled from the swimming hall back to the path.

"Enskede," she said and again laughed at him. "Where Peter and I live." She bent slightly forward and, raising her left foot behind her, away from him, began to stretch her quadriceps. She reached her right hand out toward him and rested it on his shoulder.

He steadied himself against her weight. Her hand didn't move but still seemed to pull him to her. "I'd be happy to show you some good trails here in the park," he said. He knew this would require effort on her part. She'd have to leave work or come to the city specifically to meet him. It thrilled him to test her in this way. "If you have the time," he added.

She dropped her foot to the path and raised the other, this time placing her left hand on his shoulder. Her eyes were level with his lips. "I'd like that," she said. He knew then he would be unable to keep himself away from her. She was an unknown shape in a dark room he couldn't help but reach his hand out toward.

The affair went on for three weeks before Helle agreed to sleep with him. Several times he suggested taking a room at a hotel in the city but each time he did she refused, saying she wanted to wait. For what, he didn't know. They ran together on Wednesdays. He had to slow his pace to keep from running away from her. They spoke openly and intimately on these runs and on occasion they met at the classic rock bar in the city, where it was nearly too loud to talk, but where they were certain no one either of them knew would ever come.

They shared an unhappiness that they'd only met now, after they were each married and not while they were in school and still single. In fact, they'd overlapped at Uppsala for two years. The student organization Henrik chaired had frequently hosted banquets and lectures on campus, and Helle attended many of these. There was a chance they may have met at one. It seemed almost cruel, she told him once, that they had not. When she asked him if he would have loved her had they known each other then, Henrik always answered that he would have even though he believed more in circumstance than in fate. Had they known each other under the right circumstances at Uppsala, yes, he would have loved her, but that he would have loved her then because he loved her now was, he knew, a fallacy.

In early September, Peter was selected to attend a meeting in Copenhagen and Henrik was not. Ordinarily, this would have distressed him, as it might seem to indicate his standing at work was in question, but then Helle called to ask if he was planning on attending the meeting.

"I haven't been asked to go," he told her.

"Good," she said. "Tell Lisa you have been and come to my house at seven. You'll stay the night."

He'd expected more from the house. A long crack beneath a second-floor window zigzagged down to a gray mass of dusty concrete where a piece of stucco, roughly the shape of Africa, had fallen from the wall. The flowerbed that lined the front walk needed weeding, and in the far top corner of the garage door, he saw a patch of mold-softened wood that had been sloppily painted over. He checked his watch. At precisely seven o'clock, he opened the front gate and made his way up the walk. The oak in the center of the lawn had dropped many of its leaves and he listened to his shoes grinding the dried leaves into the stones. He looked up at the tree, relieved that it was not his to clean up after. Part of the monthly fees at his apartment building covered what little yard work needed to be done there. He hadn't mowed a lawn or raked leaves since he was a child at his parents' house in Eskilstuna. Even at his summerhouse in Elmsta, he paid two local boys, twins, a thousand kronor a month to do the yard work.

At the door, he couldn't decide whether to ring the bell or knock. He settled on both, which he did in quick succession. Helle was smiling at him when she opened the door. She had on a black dress. Her hair was down. He shifted the flowers and wine he'd brought to his left hand, and kissed her hello.

Inside the house was warm, decorated simply. The walls

of the living room were white and the rug in the center of the dark hardwood floor was white. He thought the floor might be walnut. He knew very little about design but the house reminded him of something he might see on television. He felt at home. They moved farther into the house. Helle had already set the table. Various cocktail glasses and bottles had been arranged on a small table near the door between the kitchen and the dining room. She walked past the table on her way to the kitchen. With the flowers, she pointed. "Help yourself to something to drink."

Henrik poured himself a splash of scotch over a single ice cube. He sipped the scotch, taking care to pace himself, and listened to Helle bring a vase down from a cupboard and run the water. He couldn't see her but knew by the sound what she was doing. "Can I make something for you?" he said into the kitchen.

"Just wine for me, thanks," she said. "I've already opened a bottle in here." She came back into the dining room with her wine glass in one hand and the flower vase in the other. She placed the vase at the center of the dining table, adjusted its position once, stepped back from the table, paused, and stepped forward again, moving the vase slightly to the left. "They're beautiful," she said.

Henrik thought so too, though he couldn't tell what difference moving the vase had made. He took another sip of his drink. "Yes," he said.

The salmon she'd prepared was very good, and the wine she'd chosen matched the fish well. The asparagus was crisp. The potatoes reminded him of the early summer. With every bite, Henrik felt assured of his presence. He was happy to be with Helle, happy to act, however temporarily, as though they weren't hiding their relationship. Until now, it hadn't occurred to him that he'd felt any anxiety about the nature of their affair. He spent a good deal of his energy, of course, concealing it from his wife and from Peter, but he'd always known that if it became too difficult to keep up the lie he'd simply stop, which meant, now that he thought of it, he'd been unafraid to lose Helle. He hadn't at all taken her seriously. But now, in her house, he began to imagine that this could be his life. It very well could be his life. He and Lisa didn't have children. There was nothing to stop him from leaving her. She was young and attractive and had a good job. She'd find someone else. There was a man at Lisa's work, Tomas or Patrik or David, whom he knew she found attractive. Perhaps she'd already met someone of her own. This sort of thing happened all the time. People grew tired of one another.

After dinner she opened the bottle of red wine he'd brought. They moved from the dining room to the couch. More than once, Henrik looked to the table, its empty plates and flickering candles, and tried to imagine what he might be thinking five, ten years in the future when looking at a similar scene. Would he feel the same happiness? Would he remember this day? It was September tenth. Helle reminded him of the date when she brought up Anna Lindh. It was the day before the five-year anniversary of Lindh's assassination and Helle was curious, she said, to see how the media would address the issue. Anna Lindh was the foreign minister in 2003, widely expected to be next prime minister when Göran Persson's second term expired. She was stabbed to death in the NK department store while out shopping with a friend.

The music stopped playing and Helle got up from the couch to put it back on. She stood at the computer, her back to him. "Same music fine with you?

"Of course," he said. "Anything at all." He was feeling a little drunk, but pleasantly so.

"In the last five years," Helle said, returning to the couch, "there's been a change, don't you think? We're less safe." She paused here and retrieved her wine glass from the coffee table. "Or maybe it's only that we know now just how unsafe we are," she said.

She stretched her leg out toward him and rested her foot in his lap. Henrik massaged her foot with his free hand. He took a sip of his wine. After he swallowed, he said, "Well, I feel safe." He didn't mean to disagree with her, but the idea that he could feel anything other than happy at that moment seemed strange.

"That's not the point," she said. He felt the weight of her foot on his leg. Her heel pressed into his thigh. Even his shortcomings—his affair with Helle especially—had seemed to him part of the man he was supposed to be, and he'd found comfort in this. It was who he was and that felt safe. He did his best to ignore the rising anxious feeling in his chest. "The point is that the possibility exists now. Obviously, it always has. Anna Lindh was killed after all. But what I mean is, we understand now, all of us do, that such things happen. We live terrified of them every day. Even if you won't admit it."

"I can see what you mean," he said.

"It's a symbol," she said. "Our 9/11."

The day of the assassination, Henrik had been at work downtown. He'd worked for Nordea Bank then and was at the branch office next door to NK. The stabbing occurred in the late afternoon. The department store had been closed immediately and a large crowd of shoppers and office workers gathered in front. He could see them from his window. The news of Lindh's stabbing was everywhere that afternoon. Colleagues of his refreshed news websites repeatedly, eagerly shouting out any developments. Just before five, he'd left the office. He remembered being annoyed that a crowd had gathered near the scene of the murder, where very little actual information might be found, delaying his walk to the metro. He felt himself returning to that irritation. "9/11?" he said. "That's ridiculous."

Helle straightened and pulled her foot back from his lap. She smiled at him. It wasn't an unfriendly smile but it was forced. He noticed for the first time that her teeth were crooked.

"I didn't mean anything by it," he said.

"No, you're right," she said. "It's a silly comparison. Something I heard on the radio this afternoon on the way home from work." She placed her wine glass on the table.

He started to say something about the tsunami in Thailand and all the Swedish tourists who'd died there but stopped when his phone rang. He was grateful for the interruption. A colleague's name flashed across the screen. "It's Lisa," he told Helle. "I'm going to answer. She'd think it was strange if I didn't." They both rose from the couch, Helle heading toward the kitchen and Henrik to the hall. The phone continued to ring. He ended the call and held the silent phone to his ear. "This is Henrik," he said as if he were answering. Helle, holding a plate in each hand, turned and smiled at him before disappearing into the kitchen. "Yes, it's fine," he said to the phone. He concentrated on pausing long enough to give the impression that he was listening to Lisa speak. "Everything is going well. Just having dinner with Peter and some others." He knew Helle would be unable to hear him over the music. Still, he continued speaking. "My flight is at noon tomorrow. I should be home by four." Helle passed into view again. She leaned over the table and blew out the candles. He watched her leave the room with more dishes. "Yes," Henrik said, "I love you too."

On his way to the kitchen, he stopped and picked up the single remaining plate from the table. This he set on the counter beside Helle, who had begun washing the dishes. Their forks and knives were laid in a neat line on a white dishtowel next to the sink. He kissed her neck. Simple domestic gestures with Helle had always been exciting to him, more forbidden somehow than sex. "Can I help?" He reached for the towel she had over her shoulder.

"Don't," she said, placing a washed plate, facedown, to the right of the silverware. "I'm nearly done. We'll leave what's left for the morning."

He watched her rinse a few more dishes and place them on the counter as well. She slowly patted her hands dry and took a last sip of her wine before emptying the glass and setting it in the sink. Henrik placed his glass there too. He kissed her again and she smiled at him coolly.

She led him to the bedroom. She lit a candle on her bedside table. "Turn off the light," she said. He did and in the candlelight watched her shadowed figure undress in front of him. He would have liked to see her body more clearly, but felt nervous to ask for this.

They made love, and apart from a single incident in which

he pushed his elbow into her ribs and worried that he'd hurt her, he enjoyed himself and was again happy.

When they were done he lay in the warm sheets, the pillow uncomfortably tucked under his neck. The air in the room was cool. Her bed smelled unfamiliar. He'd almost fallen asleep when all at once the pain in his neck became overwhelming. He lifted his head and reached to adjust the pillow. The pain he felt and the actions he took to relieve it reminded him of the look she'd given him when he'd pressed his elbow into her ribs. They'd been on their sides and Helle turned over so that her back was to him; he moved to reposition himself on top of her, but as he did so, his arm became pinned beneath his body and hers and he slipped, putting his weight on his other elbow, which pressed into her side. She'd winced and turned to look at him.

Now he couldn't recall the pleasure of the evening. He couldn't enjoy how satisfied and enjoyably tired he felt. Instead, all he thought of was the look of pain on her face. He turned toward her and lifted himself up on his elbow. "I hope I didn't hurt you," he said.

He heard her shift to her side. She reached out to him and put her hand on his chest. "Not at all," she said. "I didn't feel anything at all." He knew she was talking about his elbow, but the idea that she might be talking about their lovemaking formed a tickle of panic in his throat and he coughed. He lay back down and didn't resist when she rested her cheek on his chest and kissed him just below his collarbone.

He slept fitfully. At 6:45 the next morning, the radio turned on to a morning political talk show. The topic of the program was the anniversary of Anna Lindh's assassination.

The panelists shared Helle's opinion from the night before that something unidentifiable but important had changed in the past five years. Every terrible accident meant something now. Every tragedy was a sign of another to come. It was a new country. And in it, no one was safe. The panelists discussed party leadership in the Social Democrats. In Anna Lindh's absence, a clear leader had still not emerged. One of the panelists attributed the conservative victory in the last election to this fact. He felt Helle begin to stir beside him. Maybe she had it right. There was something waiting for him. He didn't know what it was or when it would happen, but it was there. His thigh itched and he reached his hand beneath the duvet to scratch it. He ran his fingernail over a rough patch of skin where a drop of semen had dried to a flaky tear.

She stretched her arm out toward him and touched his shoulder. "Good morning," she said. He imagined himself getting out of bed and dressing, leaving the house with a simple apology. As he thought this, it was as though he'd already done it, and he was pleased with himself for making such a decision.

The Drowned Girl

She knew without touching the man that he was dead. And she knew without looking too closely at the bloodied hair all washed to one side that it was her neighbor Rolf Strand. He was lying in the center of the canal path near where it bent straight north and skirted the coast. Not far from Rolf's body, a bicycle was propped up at a funny angle in the dirt. From this arrangement, it was easy to see what had happened. She threw up twice onto the spongy moss beside the path.

In the days after her discovery, Ingrid had met with the police, been asked questions she didn't know how to answer. Her mother had been dead since January. A social worker came to the house. The social worker touched Ingrid's arm, said she understood, said her name was Jenny. Jenny listed words—*ice, water, bicycle*—and asked Ingrid to name the first association that came to mind. Ingrid's father watched, leaning on the peeling green wallpaper in the dim kitchen. Jenny said, "Tree." Ingrid said, "Tree." When it was over, Jenny smiled and left the room with Ingrid's father. She heard them whispering at the front door. "Not for now," she heard. "Time heals all wounds," she heard. Everyone in the village, her father, the police, her brothers, they all spoke to her slowly, stepped too far away, as if she were an object they were afraid to break.

She hardly spoke that summer. Her father gave her tasks. She learned to cook simple meals. She cleaned the house every week. She sailed with her brothers in the sun-cracked dinghy. When they tried to go out far, she gripped the boat's rail until they turned back.

The first storms of fall helped. She began to hope for them.

On All Saints' Day, she stood at the tall window in the front room and watched a storm tumble in from the east. The twins, Eskil and Einar, were chopping wood for the furnace. She heard their laughter and the ax splitting the wood. The dark line of the storm's approaching shadow stretched across the water. Ingrid had planned to make her mother's favorite meal—baked whitefish fresh from the fisherman—to celebrate her mother. They'd never observed All Saints' Day before, because they had never had anyone to remember. The rain would make the walk to the fisherman cold and wet. Through the window, she watched the clouds swell.

The ax fell again, and again a log split. Her brothers were making good progress. She looked at the clock. It was a quarter to four in the afternoon. Her father had promised to be home by five. He'd gone to the village for wine and groceries. Nearly every night she heard her father drunkenly whisper prayers.

Ingrid's mother was buried in the tree-filled cemetery of the small church out on the stubby peninsula on the island's southeast corner. Ingrid and her father planned to drive to the cemetery and place a grave candle at the headstone.

She pulled a sweater on over her head. It was one of her mother's old sweaters but no longer smelled like her mother. Ingrid's mother had drowned in the icy water of the Baltic while out skating on the thin sea ice. There'd been a warm stretch of days, each starting with a warning from the municipal authorities about the thinning ice. But her mother insisted on going out. She was training for a trip she took every February with her skating club to the frozen rivers of Norrland. That day they'd planned to cover ten kilometers, out and back. They'd kept close to the shore, and had seen no reason to use the safety lines. Ingrid imagined the accident so often it had become a memory. The water seeping up through the ice, the long strokes of her mother's legs closing the distance at great speed. The ice cracked, moaned, cracked again. The splashed water from her mother's flailing arms, the shouting, the panicked call on the cell phone for help. It took a team of divers three hours to recover the body.

By spring, her mother had disappeared from the house. First it was her clothes, then her books, and her jewelry, the serving dishes Ingrid knew her parents had been given as a wedding present. Her father had put all of her mother's belongings in boxes and stacked them in neat rows in the small building up on the rocky hill behind the house. The building had once been a guest cottage. When she was very young, Ingrid used to play there. Sometimes at night, she watched the windows of the cottage lit dimly around her father's grieving silhouette.

She left through the back door so her brothers wouldn't see her. She planned to walk to the fisherman and buy two whitefish. The clouds were dark and heavy over the water. She knew she would not beat the rain. She moved quickly around the house and down the front path. The sea was whitecapped, the road ahead of her dark. Behind her she heard her brothers laughing and the ax dropping into the chopping block and the hollow sound of split logs being thrown atop already-split logs.

His arm weighed three kilograms. To figure this out, Fredrik Holm weighed himself twice, once with the arm on and once with it off. When he was finished he replaced the scale in its spot beside the toilet. He left the arm resting on the sink. Without the arm, he felt out of balance. The orthopedic specialist assured him this displaced equilibrium would pass, but it had been nearly a year since he lost his arm and the sensation had yet to decrease. He looked at his reflection in the bathroom mirror, turning to block his incomplete half. In spite of his best efforts to conceal his disability, it was impossible to mask the sharp dip of his left shoulder and the effect this had on his posture.

Outside, the rainwater poured steadily from the broken gutter above the bedroom window. Tomas, the Polish man who lived in the village, would repair it if only Fredrik called. Fredrik disliked asking for help. He heard the water slapping into a muddy puddle.

From the window, he stared out at the storm. The thick air, heavy with rain, clung to the water's surface. A young girl was walking up his front path, a large white sweater hanging over her small body. It was Ingrid Källström, the girl who discovered Rolf Strand's body in June. Fredrik and Rolf had played their weekly tennis match the day of the accident. Fredrik lost. After the match, Rolf had bicycled away from the courts. Fredrik stayed behind to talk with Manne Björnsson, a neighbor from Stockholm whose own summerhouse wasn't far from Fredrik's, and who often reserved the court after Rolf and Fredrik had played. By the time they'd finished their conversation the drawbridge was up and Fredrik was left to wait on the mainland side of the village before continuing his walk home. A quarter of an hour later, after he'd crossed the drawbridge, he heard the siren of an approaching ambulance. He wouldn't know until later that evening that it had anything to do with his friend. He sometimes wondered what the siren would have sounded like to him if he had.

The girl stopped beside the tall birch, the roots of which had begun to lift and crack the stones of his front path. She looked up at the house and before he could release the curtain, he saw that she saw him looking out at her from the window. She waved, then jogged up the path and stepped onto his front porch. He had never spoken to Ingrid. She knocked. He considered not opening the door. She knocked again and said, loudly, "May I stand on your porch until it stops raining?"

He opened the door and smiled at her. "You'd better come inside," he said.

She waited in the kitchen while he fetched a towel. Two small puddles formed at her feet.

He placed the towel on the kitchen table. "Help yourself," he said. The wind blew hard off the water, rattling the shutters. It was cold. He understood why she stopped to wait out the storm. Two years before, a branch from the tall birch in his front yard was torn from the tree by heavy winds. The branch fell on his car, denting the roof and shattering one of the back windows.

Ingrid was holding a bag. More precisely, she was holding a paper bag inside of a plastic bag. Björn, the fisherman from around the point, packaged his fish this way. Fredrik reached out his right hand to take the bags from her. She dried her hair in the towel.

When he turned back to Ingrid, she held it close to her chest. She was staring at his stooped left side. "Thank you," she said.

It was then he realized he was not wearing his arm. "You're very welcome," he said. "It's wet out."

"I thought I could beat the storm," she said. As if she suddenly understood that she'd been staring at his shoulder, she shifted awkwardly from one foot to the other and looked down at the table.

The rain was falling hard onto the puddled walk. "It came quick today," he said. "Would you like some coffee?"

She looked at him, smiled. "I'm not old enough," she said, folding the towel loosely in half and draping it over the arm of the low club chair he kept in the space between the dining area and the living room. The chair was leather but worn and very old. It had been his father's. He looked at the wet towel. There was a time when he'd have flinched at a wet towel on the chair but that time was long since gone.

"Of course," he said. "No, of course."

He put the kettle on for tea. From the cupboard beside the refrigerator, he took out a tin of shortbread cookies Rolf had brought from a trip to England six months before he died. He set the tin on the table and after struggling to remove the top said, "If you can open it, help yourself to a cookie."

The kettle whistled. She flinched at the sound. Several times he announced that it was still raining out. Each time he did, Ingrid agreed. He hadn't thought much about Ingrid past those first hurried and hectic days after Rolf's accident. He'd heard about her mother, of course. The whole village talked about it through March. Still an occasional mention at the ICA or at the bar near the drawbridge. An avoidable accident, they all said. A waste. So young. Here in his kitchen was the closest he'd been to Ingrid. She looked somewhat different from his idea of her. She was so young, not more than thirteen or fourteen, he guessed, but he had no grandchildren of his own with which to compare. He knew by the shape of her face that she would one day be a beautiful woman. The warmth of the teacup in his hand reminded him of its presence. He raised the cup to his lips, blew away a thin blossom of steam, and sipped the tea.

"The fish is for my father," Ingrid said. Her voice was soft, almost a whisper.

"He shouldn't have let you walk out in this storm."

"He went to town to do the shopping," she said.

"Would you like me to drive you home?"

"The rain will stop soon," she said. "Thank you. I should have said thank you first." She lifted her teacup to her mouth and set it down again without drinking. When she pulled her hand away from the mug, a splash of tea dribbled over the lip and down to the table. She tried to wipe it away with her hand. "What happened to your arm?" she asked. "People tell stories but I don't believe any of them."

Fredrik touched his shoulder, looked away in the direction of the bathroom. "I have a disease called diabetes," he said finally. "This disease sometimes causes vascular problems. Do you know what that word means?"

"I don't know," she said, still wiping at the wet spot with her fingers.

He wanted to get up and get a kitchen towel for her but didn't want her to think he was embarrassed to talk about his arm. "It means the veins," he said. "Blood."

"And so they had to take your arm?"

"Our bodies betray us," he said and regretted the seriousness of the comment.

Ingrid got up from her chair and crossed the room to get the towel she'd used earlier to dry her hair. Above the chair, pictures from his tennis career, spaced unevenly and dense, hung on the worn white wall. He'd liked the spot because the pictures were present and when he felt like it he could revisit those years, but he could just as easily ignore them too. She put a knee on the chair and pushed herself up to get a better look at the photographs. "Is this a picture of you when you were young?"

The photograph was taken in 1967 at a tennis tournament in Massachusetts. It was the first time he'd been to America. After the longest match he ever played, Fredrik won the tournament. It was his first win. His winnings paid for the summerhouse.

"It's me," he said.

"I didn't know you were a tennis player," she said. "No one ever tells children the truth."

"It was a short career and I don't talk much about it. That photograph was taken after the last match I won." He got up and joined Ingrid at the chair, taking a half step to the side of the chair and leaning slightly against the arm.

Ingrid pushed, almost imperceptibly, away from him. He knew he'd made her uncomfortable. He took the picture off the wall and returned with it to the table.

"Did you like being a tennis player?" Ingrid asked. She sat down opposite him. "My father makes me take lessons every summer but I'm not very good."

"They didn't have TV cameras everywhere in those days and there wasn't so much money," he looked up from the photograph. "I'm sure you're better than you think."

"My brothers say I don't try hard enough."

"Brothers like to say such things."

"Especially mine," she said.

"I only played for three seasons," he said. "I quit right after this picture was taken."

"Why?"

"I was tired and wanted to rest. As soon as I got back to Sweden, I told my coaches I was taking a vacation. It was several weeks until the next tournament I'd planned on entering. So I went to Greece for a month. I told everyone I wanted to celebrate. But I knew I was quitting." He stopped and looked at Ingrid and then continued when she smiled at him, encouragingly. "I took a room on the island of Paros in a little hotel full of West Germans and English," he continued. "Everyone was scared of the communists in those days. It seems so silly to think about now. Have you ever visited Greece?"

"Once when I was little we went. I don't remember any of it." She dabbed at what was left of the tea with the towel. He looked away from this, pretended not to notice. That trip to Greece was the first time he'd seen a dead body. He was

much older than Ingrid was, ten years at least. He felt himself starting to tell her about it, even though he knew he
shouldn't. It was like being slightly drunk at a dinner party
and speaking too openly with someone he hardly knew, a
feeling he knew well.

"My first day, I went to the beach at Kolympithres. It was
crowded, and incredibly hot. You wouldn't believe how hot.
I had a hard time finding a place to lie down and was about
to go back to my room when I saw a large group of people
gathered at one end of the beach. I walked over to see why.
The day before, a man at the hotel had told me about a dol-
phin that had beached itself earlier in the summer and died. I
wondered whether something like that had happened again."

The storm was passing, moving quickly inland. He knew
this by the changing light in through the small window above
the sink.

"As I got closer to the group of people," he said, "I saw
that there was a young woman lying in the sand. Her wet
hair clung to her face and fanned out across the sand beneath her head. I understood right away that she'd drowned."
Ingrid sat rigidly in her chair, looking down at her hands on
the table. He remembered the day so vividly. The crowd had
stood around the body for a long time. He'd stayed there too,
curious about what would happen, maybe a little curious to
see how long he could stand it. Finally, someone picked up a
towel from the sand nearby, shook it out, and covered the body.
The towel didn't reach the woman's feet. It stopped midway
down her calf. Her legs were tan and the bottoms of her feet
were extremely white. "I'm sorry," he said. "I shouldn't have
told you any of that. I'd only meant to tell you about my

tennis days. Well." Fredrik put the photograph down on the table. Its frame clapped loudly against the wood.

Ingrid, her body no less rigid, leaned into the table so that her chest met the edge. She said, "My mother drowned."

"I know," he said. "I didn't mean to hurt your feelings." The light coming in through the window had intensified, its lines sharper and the shadow between the refrigerator and the counter darker.

"We have to visit her grave and light a candle tonight," she said.

"That's a nice tradition," he said. "When I'm in the city I do that for my mother, too."

Later, after they'd finished their tea and she'd thanked him for the towel, he showed her to the door and watched as she stepped around a small puddle where the stones had receded to a shallow divot that was filled with water. At the end of the path, she turned to wave and he waved back. He kept his arm raised until she disappeared around the first bend in the road. The clouds were moving quickly and above the water the sky was clear.

The house was out of sight by the time she remembered the fish. The bag was still on the counter beside the refrigerator. She wasn't far from the house and could go back easily, but the thought of doing so produced a tickle in her throat. She coughed twice into her hand and didn't go back.

Her father was unloading the groceries from the trunk of the car when she came up the road to the house. He placed a bag in her arms. "When I called, the boys told me you'd gone," her father said. "I kept an eye out for you on my drive home but I didn't see you."

"Here I am," she said.

"They did a good job," he said and pointed to the neatly stacked wood.

Her father prepared chicken for dinner, and they did not speak about her mother.

After dark, she and her father drove to the cemetery. Eskil and Einar stayed at home. In the car, her father said he was too tired to fight with them. The church parking lot was full of cars and the only available spot was in the center of a large puddle. Her father let her out before he parked. She watched the car ease into the puddle, water lifting and cresting away from the tires. The red brake lights were reflected in the black water. Her father opened the door and stepped, first a long, slow step and then two quick steps out of the water, to the muddy gravel of the parking lot.

She followed her father to the grave. The grass was wet and slippery and the paths were pocked with footprints. It was silent apart from the wind and the footfalls of other visitors.

Her father read her mother's name aloud from the headstone. He started to say the dates of birth and death but stopped before he'd finished. She could tell he didn't know what to do.

"Say a prayer," she said.

He began to recite the Lord's Prayer but stopped after the first few lines. "I don't know the rest," he said. "I thought it'd come to me but it didn't."

They stood at the grave for a long time. She carefully relit the candle when it extinguished in a gust. It was late and the wind that earlier cleared the sky brought the biting cold air off the water. Her father put his arm around her and pulled her to him, briskly rubbing his hand over her shoulder. "She was a good mother," he said, "and a good wife. We miss you." He reached out and touched the top of the headstone with his fingertips.

The crisp reflections of the trees and the candlelight and her and her father's legs shook in the rippling puddles. They walked quickly back to the car. The wind was at their backs.

They joined the line of cars leaving the parking lot. The windows had fogged and through the palled glass she watched the red brake lights ahead extinguish and light again as the cars edged forward.

The drive was short but felt long. Not far from the church, the road reached the water and followed the coastline nearly all the way to their house. Ingrid watched the water, the steady pattern of whitecaps moving toward land. When they reached the house, her father turned into their drive. The headlights illuminated a shape on the front step. She knew what it was. Though she'd done nothing wrong and might easily explain the afternoon, she hurried to reach the bag before her father could. She heard his footsteps behind her. "Ingrid," he said, "what's wrong?"

She took the bag from the step and moved into the porch light to look more closely. Fredrik had folded a small yellow piece of paper in half and stapled it to the bag. She opened the paper and saw that he'd written, in small letters, her name. "What is that?" her father asked. He reached for the bag, but she turned away from him.

"Fish," she said. "It's fish." She heard the water in the shallow inlet opposite the house. Rolf Strand's boat was still moored there with a rusty spring line to a moss-covered rock. The boat pulled against the line, bumped back into the rock, pulled against the line again. She listened to this rhythm. She heard her father's voice speaking to her and the voices of her brothers inside coming closer to the door. The voices and the hollow thumping of the empty boat against the rock were the gathered crowd and Ingrid was the drowned girl. She felt the sand on her back and the wind on her tender white feet. She looked down the dark road. The tall thin birches swallowed it whole in the windy night. From out of the darkness she saw him, young, two-armed, sunburned, and handsome, approaching.

Henrik Needed Help

From the bottom of a shallow ditch, Henrik needed help. From inside his car at the bottom of the shallow ditch beside the southbound lane, he needed help. From where he was seat-belted to the driver's seat of his upside-down Volvo, he needed help. It was late, and Jenny was driving south, listening to a radio documentary about North Korea. She saw the cast of bright headlights out of the shallow ditch. She saw a ghostly cloud rising from the shallow ditch. Up the road, she saw in the wash of her own headlights tire marks disappearing into the shallow ditch. Henrik's phone was in his computer bag in the backseat of the car. His phone was in his computer bag on the ceiling of the upturned car. His phone was unreachable because his arm was pinned between his body and the crumpled door. He needed help for the injuries to his

body. He needed help for his broken arm, for his cracked pel-
vis, for his crushed ribs, for his shattered jaw. He needed help
for a broken finger. In his mind, he visited a warm and sunny
beach. He remembered the sound of the pages of his wife
Lisa's magazine in the wind. He thought he heard a car come
to a stop on the shoulder above him. He thought he heard a
car come to a stop on the shoulder above him and a car door
slam shut and the dry rain of rocks falling into the shallow
ditch. His eyes were open. The gravel avalanched beneath her.
What if a child was in the car? What if an injured child was
in the car? What if a dead child was in the car? He thought
he heard someone calling out to him, though he did not hear
his name. It was July but already there was steam from the
exhaust. He thought he saw a deer. He thought he saw a deer
and swerved to avoid it. He thought he saw a deer peering in
at him from outside. Jenny was not a deer. She was here to
help. She said something from the dark outside. There was
no child in the car. There was only a man in the car. There
was blood painted onto the cracked window glass. A pair of
legs was in the light. A pair of legs took two steps closer. A
pair of legs became a single leg beyond the dented frame of
the shattered windshield. "Are you alive?" asked Jenny. "Can
you hear me?" she said. Henrik's body was failing. His body
was frightening. His body was a body. He wanted to know if
he had died. He wanted to know what he did to deserve this.
But he knew this is what had been waiting.

Ships of Stockholm

A group of tourists were pointing and taking photographs of the building with the stone sculpture of a vulva carved into the acanthus leaf cornice above the entryway. Lennart watched this. He smelled the brackish water and the sharp sting of diesel coming at him in the wind off the bay. It was the first Tuesday in July, a week after his father died, and the city was crowded with tourists and locals off work for summer vacation. The sun was out and the day was warm.

At Slussen, he put three ten-kronor coins in a graffiti-covered vending machine for a copy of *DN*, and sat on a bench, warmed by the sun, near the center of the square. It was summer and the news was slow. He scanned headlines about outbreaks of stomach viruses on cruise ships, and the wedding of a Scottish footballer who'd briefly played in Sweden. Light, inconsequential stuff, all of it. He read half an article about rats. The mild winter had allowed an infestation to develop in some government buildings.

He was late for a meeting with his father's lawyer. Matilda, his younger sister, was probably already there, as were Ulrika and Magnus, his older siblings. Matilda lived in the city, but the other two had come from abroad to be in Stockholm for the meeting. Lennart had started to go, but the thought of sitting around a conference room table in a cramped office, listening to his father's stern lawyer list assets and properties and tax liabilities, dug into him and his head hurt. The office walls were crowded with cheap prints of bad artwork, idyllic Nordic landscapes made claustrophobic and menacing behind dusty plastic frames. And the furniture was too bland, bureaucratic for the austere old-town space the office occupied. The place always made Lennart a little sad.

Someone at the lawyer's office called twice. Soon after the second call, his sister started calling. Each time, he watched her name flash on the screen until it stopped. From the bench, he had a clear view of the bay. Steam rose from the stacks of one of the Silja Line cruise ships. It had been years since he'd been on one of the Baltic cruises. Once, when he was young, not more than ten as he remembered it, he and his father had gone to Finland for a couple of days, just the two of them. His father had some business in Helsinki. On the return trip, Lennart had been allowed to play one of the electronic slot machines. Even at ten, he knew he wasn't supposed to do this. The machine his father picked was tucked away from the sight of the casino attendant, partially blocking a small window completely blackened with the night. Rolf had stood close behind, obscuring any view of Lennart pressing

the buttons on the screen. Lennart fed a hundred-kronor bill
into the machine and watched as the screen came to life with
a brightly colored set of images of fruit and gold coins and
treasure chests, all connected by a complicated web of blinking lines. On his second spin, the machine hit the jackpot,
and a happy-sounding but deafening bell rang out. His father
clapped him cheerfully on the back and quickly took Lennart
down from the stool he'd been perched on. Rolf had had to
walk into the casino to fetch someone to arrange for the pay-
out and left Lennart at the machine, the bell still sounding
and the word *winner* flashing on the screen. He sat transfixed
by this and by his own fear of being found out, of his father
getting in some kind of trouble.

Finally, his father returned with an attendant, a rough-
looking guy with bursts of red veins flowering out across his
cheeks from too much drinking. He looked at Lennart, messed
his hair. "Good luck charm," the attendant said in a thick Finnish accent. Then he gave Rolf a slip with the amount of their
winnings. They'd only won five hundred kronor but his father
had let him keep the money, a small kindness that Lennart
often returned to much later when he and his father had had
an argument, something that happened frequently even into
Lennart's adulthood.

His sister called again. Again he ignored the call. He
decided he'd like to have a drink. There were plenty of bars
along Götgatan but Lennart passed each of them on his way
to the terrace at Mosebacke, the bar behind the Söder Theater.
He wanted to sit outside, and the bar was a large outdoor terrace high up on a cliff overlooking the water, picnic tables
arranged along the edges of the terrace and foosball and Ping-
Pong tables in the center. All the seating at Mosebacke was

full. He circled the terrace looking for a group that might soon be done. On his second pass, a woman sitting near the edge of the terrace smiled at him. "You're welcome to join me," she said in English. She was holding a Stockholm tour book and waved it at him. "I was just reading." She laughed and smiled at him. There was a good view of the water from the table.

Lennart thanked her and sat down. She pointed to his drink. "I didn't know you had to go to the bar to be served. I sat here for ages waiting." She laughed and shook her head at this. Lennart couldn't place her accent exactly, but it was American.

"It's a lovely city," the woman said. The umbrella in the center of the table was closed. Its crisp shadow reached across the table and onto the woman's chest and face. She sounded affected in a way he thought she meant to indicate she was the sort of person who traveled, had been places. He often met such people when he lived in North Carolina. Doctors and university professors who had visited France once and pronounced the names of each village they'd visited in exaggerated ways. "Everywhere I've been has been so crowded. Yesterday I followed a Chinese tour group around the modern museum for an hour. I didn't learn anything but the art was lovely. An artist named Mamma Andersson. I bought a poster. Do you know her work?"

Lennart's phone rang.

The woman raised her book. "Oh, sorry," she mouthed. "Go ahead."

It was his sister again. He rejected the call, and put the phone on top of the newspaper in front of him, waiting to see what the woman might say next. "Are you enjoying your stay?" he asked after she didn't say anything for a little while. He immediately regretted the simplicity of the question.

"It's so beautiful here," the woman said. "The Venice of the north. Is that what people call it or just the tour books? It seems like a fair comparison. I've never been to Venice, though."

"It's the water," he said. "Islands and so on." He had the feeling that a conversation with the woman could take any turn at all, and he liked this, the possibilities it presented. He was also attracted to her. She was pretty, if plain, but more than that, he was drawn to where the afternoon might end if he let it. His phone buzzed. On the screen, a message indicating that he had a voicemail flashed brightly. He deleted the message.

"You're busy," the woman said, touching her chest, below her neck, where the skin was freckled, "and I just keep going on and on." She returned to her book, quickly thumbing through the pages. He watched her read. Soon he was distracted by all the movement below in the bay. There were dozens of boats and ferries. A roller coaster at the Gröna Lund amusement park crested the top of its track. He looked from this back to the woman. He sipped his beer. She wasn't the sort of woman he normally found attractive. She was older than he was, or at least looked older than he was, and though he was of course only speculating about it, she seemed to have a sadness about her that was far more complicated than he was interested in sharing or even tolerating—a messy divorce, a dead kid, recovering drug addict, something like that. But still, there it was, this attraction, undeniable, present in spite of his attempts to ignore it. He wanted to reach out and take her hand.

"I keep interrupting you," the woman said. She looked up from her book and turned it so that it faced Lennart. "But am I reading the map properly? I think I am but it's hard to tell. All the water. And the jet lag. I slept all morning. Coming this way, east I guess it'd be, is the worst."

He pushed his phone and the newspaper out of the way so the woman could place the book in front of him. "What are you trying to find?" he said. He knew the city well. Here was a problem he could fix.

The woman pointed to the map. "The Vasa Museum," she said. "That's it there, right?" She tapped her finger on the map and then pointed across the bay, leaning to try to see the museum. Lennart didn't think it was possible to see it from this side of Skeppsholmen, even from high up at the terrace.

"Yes," said Lennart, a little disappointed that what she was looking for was close, so easy to point to. "It's just beyond the island there, the larger of the two. You can't see it from here, but it's on the far side. Can't miss it." He had meant to suggest that he take her there himself later that afternoon, but now that he'd explained how easy it was to find, he'd need to come up with something better. The *Vasa* was accidentally rediscovered when the channel in the bay was dredged to accommodate the increasingly large cruise liners that came in and out of Stockholm. Centuries of mud and silt preserved the ship and now, exposed to the air, it was slowly crumbling.

"I'm only here for a week," the woman said. "Would you recommend touring? I've already been to a number of museums." She didn't wear any jewelry and had slender fingers that moved quickly from object to object in a way that Lennart thought was inelegant but attractive. He'd been to the Vasa many times. The ship rested on a group of metal pylons arranged at the bottom of a dry dock in the center of the building. The main hall always smelled damp, thick with tar. The ship was remarkable in size, but only because it was indoors and so old.

"I haven't been in years," he said. "My father took my sister and me to the opening—1989, that must have been." The *Vasa* sank in 1628 on her maiden voyage. He'd always remembered historical dates easily but not those from his own life. One summer when Lennart was a boy, not long after the trip with his father, a heavy storm had hit the island where his father had his summerhouse and flooded the house, seawater reaching all the way inland to the village that straddled the canal between the island and the mainland. He remembered the rain lasting days. The night after his father died, Lennart had been unable to sleep. What kept him awake wasn't the grief of losing his father, at least not exactly. It was the question of whether the storm had occurred the summer before or the summer after his parents divorced. He'd been at the house, he thought, but had his father? Had his mother? The storm held greater symbolic meaning if it happened the year before the divorce, but he couldn't be sure he wasn't forcing that meaning to exist where there was none. But what difference did it make? The storm was neither a sign of things to come, nor the result of the past. It was heavy rain and waves that broke high on the shore, flowed into the house, carried his father's boat away. There was no meaning. It just happened.

"It must have been quite the ordeal," the woman said.

Obviously, she meant the museum opening itself, not his father's having taken him to it, but the inclination to respond literally itched coarsely in his throat. He tried to recall if it had been an ordeal. There must have been some sort of celebration, but he couldn't locate a clear memory of the day he'd gone, and his father disliked crowds so it was unlikely they'd gone to a ribbon cutting or a parade. For as long as Lennart could remember, the fact that he had gone to the opening of the Vasa Museum had been a fact of his life. To revisit the memory had never occurred to him. "I guess I don't remember," he said.

The woman looked down at her guidebook and Lennart followed her eyes to an image of the three familiar stylized masts rising from the boxy red building. "The architecture looks gorgeous," she said "Where I'm from in Chicago there are tours you can take just to learn about architecture. I've never been but I hear they are very informative."

"I don't think we have anything like that here," Lennart said.

"No," the woman said as if to confirm the fact. "That's too bad."

Lennart's phone buzzed again. A text message from his sister: "Where are you? We're waiting. M & U are pissed. Answer me?" He deleted the message.

"What do you do?" the woman asked suddenly. Though he lived in the United States for a long time, it always took him a moment to understand that when Americans asked this they were asking about work.

"I'm an engineer for a mobile telephone company," he said, a little disappointed he hadn't thought of something else to tell her, art historian, gastroenterologist, minister of education, anything.

"And you're skipping out on work?" she said, starting to laugh. "That must be why your phone keeps ringing."

"Summer holiday," he said, raising his glass. "I have full permission to drink during the day."

She raised her empty glass at him. Beyond her he could just make out the small figures of people lined up in the glass-walled gangway attached to a cruise ship's hull farther down the wharf. On the water, there were ferries and motorboats. It was a nice day to be out on the water. In North Carolina, he'd once been in love with a woman who'd claimed people have eleven senses. Everyone was mistaken that there were only five, she'd told him. It was so limiting, so inhuman. There were four different types of touch: pain, cold, pressure, and heat. Then there was taste, sight, hearing, smell, balance, and acceleration. And finally kinesthetic sense, which is the ability to locate various body parts (the shoulder, for example) when not looking at them. His phone buzzed.

"Working vacation?" He watched her eyes dart quickly to his empty beer glass and then back up to him.

"It's nothing serious," he said. "Just something I don't want to do." Once, he must have been in fourth or fifth grade, he told his friend Conny that his father beat him. He'd wanted to see how Conny would react. Lennart often lied just to see what might happen.

"Turn off the phone. Enjoy the day," the woman said. She raised her glass, sipped from it, and looked away.

Lennart turned toward the bar, looking for one of the waitresses so that he could order drinks. "You're right," he said and turned back to the woman. He felt the gentle rub of the alcohol brush against the inside of his stomach, rising pleasurably. He was happy and hopeful about the afternoon, and about his father, and his siblings. Let them wait, let them make a decision for once. He turned to the woman and said, more weakly than he'd meant, "Perhaps I can show you the museum."

"Look at that," the woman said. She pointed to the water with her empty wine glass.

In the bay, only a finger or two from shore when seen from the distance of the terrace, a passenger ferry had caught on fire. Flames clawed the fore section of the boat. They jumped and pulsed, lipped over the top of the pilot's cabin. A steady cloud of black smoke rose up and outward, obscuring parts of the ferry and the passengers racing madly across its decks. Lennart was surprised he'd missed the commotion until then. Gusts of wind pushed the smoke toward land, forming a long tubular cloud. He leaned forward across the table toward the woman for a clearer view. "I hope no one's hurt," she said flatly. "It looks bad."

Three white lifeboats drifted slowly away from the flames in the direction of the crowd of boats that had by now circled the ferry. From the terrace, it was only possible to see a raised arm, an upright torso, a blur of color from panicked movement. Most of the people at the bar had come to stand at the wall, drinks in hand, conversations lost. He felt knees pressing into his back as people strained to watch the fire. More boats circled in the water. A firefighting boat raced in from the east.

"I've never seen anything like this," the woman said.

A person jumped from the boat to the water. Lennart placed both of his hands out to steady himself against the table. The woman put her hands on top of his. Her hands were warm and the table was warm from the sun. One of the enormous Viking Line ships, inbound from the archipelago, approached, its passengers unaware of the tragedy they would soon witness.

Lennart's phone rang again. It vibrated loudly against the table. He started to reach for the phone. The woman gripped his hands tighter. "Don't," she said. "Everything is going to be fine."

In the Night of the Day Before

Martin was in a private room at the Sakura Karaoke Bar with fifteen people who worked for him. "Hotel California" was next on the list. The song's title blinked on the small television screen. Behind the title, cherry blossoms bloomed in time-lapse. Sandra, his secretary, had made him promise that he'd sing "Hotel California." Martin was retiring and Sandra had arranged a night out to celebrate. She'd invited Martin's whole department and they'd all come, which Martin appreciated. Even Lennart, who'd only just started at the Stockholm office, had made it. Martin's wife, Louise, had not wanted to come and he was happy for that.

Sandra picked the song because Martin had once been to California. That was before he started working for Ericsson. He'd been sent for a training course. The course was in Los

Angeles, though the company was located in Silicon Valley. After the course had finished, he stayed in California through the end of the week. He rented a car and drove north from Los Angeles on Highway 1, which everyone at the course told him he should drive. He was excited to visit San Francisco. It was a city he thought he knew well from television. Highway 1 was very beautiful but the driving was slow.

In San Luis Obispo, he met a young man at a bar. The young man said his name was Cesar and spoke with an accent Martin had never heard before. He knew Cesar would ask for money eventually, but Martin was on vacation and certain he deserved this, so he put the thought of money out of his mind and thought instead of Cesar's tanned face and slender wrists. He had difficulty understanding what Cesar was saying in the loud bar. The bar was on Chorro Street, not far from Mission San Luis Obispo. The broad white walls of the mission were yellow under the streetlights when he and Cesar walked past it to his motel.

From the window of the room, there was a view of Highway 1. Cesar undressed and Martin watched this and also the headlights that flashed in through the gap between the wall and the thick floral-patterned curtains he'd drawn immediately after entering the room.

When it was over, he lay awake and listened to Cesar breathe. Cesar's chest was smooth except for a small patch of coarse black hair and Martin watched this move with each breath. A vein in Cesar's neck pulsed steadily. Martin reached out and put his fingertips softly on it. He felt the flutter of the boy's blood, the rise and fall of his chest.

The next morning, he woke up to an empty bed. He'd expected this. A piece of yellow paper had been ripped out of a brochure for wine tasting on the central coast and lay on top of Martin's wallet, two of the ripped edges beginning to curl in the heat. On the piece of paper, Cesar had written: "Thanks." Under this word, he'd drawn a small heart. Martin tossed the paper into the trash can.

It was just before nine. He showered and dressed. Then he made the bed, pulling the top sheet tight across the yellowed bottom sheet and tucking the comforter in between the bed and the wall. The pillows were uneven lumps. He looked at the bed and knew that the housekeeper would have to undo his work, but making the bed was a habit he could not break. He checked out early.

Over a cup of coffee from a McDonald's he watched two pigeons fight over a hamburger wrapper in the parking lot. Then he continued driving north, but now along 101. He passed through cities with names like Atascadero and Paso Robles. He pronounced the name of each city aloud as he passed. He didn't know whether he was saying the words correctly. By that afternoon, he was in San Francisco. He checked in to the Holiday Inn on Van Ness, and requested a room on the top floor. From his room, he could see the bay and the blinking red lights on the towers of the Bay Bridge, which he mistakenly assumed was the Golden Gate.

He ate dinner at the restaurant bar. The halibut was dry. The bartender claimed it was caught that afternoon, but Martin didn't believe this. He avoided looking at the other guests.

In the morning, he took the ferry to Alcatraz. On board, he bought a ticket for the prison tour. The boat ride was choppy and cold. He stayed inside the passenger cabin and watched the waves and the seagulls that hovered about the boat.

On the island, he saw the barracks and admired a dilapi-
dated water tower. Ivy grew up its trellis and over the rusted
supports and into the rotting wooden base of the tank. The
wind was blowing hard from what seemed like all directions
at once. There was a whole city on Alcatraz, abandoned to
disuse and decay. He walked past foundations and former
garden plots and two rusted metal kitchen chairs resting on
their backs at the foot of a thick bush.

Inside the prison, he volunteered to demonstrate captiv-
ity for the group. A nervous woman named Melanie, whose
daughter had pushed her forward when the tour guide asked
for volunteers, joined him in the cell. Melanie answered
"Salinas" when the tour guide asked where she was from. The
two of them entered the cell and turned to face the group.
The tour guide asked Martin what his name was. He looked
at the small crowd of people outside the cell and he looked
at the tour guide. Then he said, "My name is Robert."

Then the tour guide asked Martin where he was from.
He said, "Stockholm." And then added, "In Sweden." The cell
door rolled into place.

The tour guide told the group to imagine what life would
have been like for the prisoners. "This is no Salinas," the guide
said. "No Stockholm." Martin held a cell bar in each of his
hands. They were cold and rough. On the back wall of the cell
a small hole through which a prisoner had once escaped. The
tour guide recited a brief explanation of how the prisoner had
created the hole and concealed it from the prison guards.

Then the tour guide made a big show of setting Martin
and the woman free from jail. "Melanie," he said, and smiled at
the group. "You served your time." The tour guide then turned
to Martin. "Stockholm," he said. "You are rehabilitated." The

tour guide then pulled a lever at the end of the block of cells and the door opened. When Martin stepped free from the cell, the tour guide leaned forward and whispered, "I'm sorry. I forgot your name."

On the ferry back to Pier 33, Melanie approached him. Her daughter was behind her, nodding her head in an encouraging way. "Hello," Melanie said. She took a seat beside him and held out her hand for him to shake. He took her hand, shook it, and said, again, "My name is Robert." He pronounced Robert the American way. He thought this would make it easier for Melanie to understand him. She said the name back to him. It sounded unnatural to him and he regretted immediately not giving her his real name. "We were locked up together," she said.

"Yes," he said. Melanie appeared not to have planned what to say after this. She sat and looked at her shoes. This made him uncomfortable, so he asked her what her and her daughter's plans for the rest of the day were. Outside, the whitecaps stretched across the bay. There was a thick fog sitting beyond the bridge.

"Forbes Island," she said. "I saw a program about it and have always wanted to go. Do you know what it is?"

He said that he did not.

"It's a houseboat, or more of a barge, really," Melanie said. She looked to her daughter as if for confirmation. "I don't know. It's a floating island. There's a restaurant there."

The ferry landed. Melanie and her daughter disembarked before he did. They were waiting for him when he got off the boat. The wind was still blowing, but he was now able to feel that it blew in off the water. "My daughter is going back to our hotel to do some schoolwork," Melanie said. "I was thinking a glass of wine at Forbes sounded pretty good about now. Care to join me?"

Melanie's daughter looked at him and said, as though he had accused her of not knowing, "The hotel is just over there."

"Yes," he said. "I'd like that." He watched Melanie's daughter walk away from them, her hair blowing with the wind away from the water and toward the city. Soon he and Melanie were walking slowly in the opposite direction along the busy and wide sidewalk of the Embarcadero.

"There used to be sea lions here," Melanie said. They'd come to Pier 39. Even in the late afternoon it was busy with tourists and traffic. Martin disliked crowds. "But they're all gone now for some reason. The guide on our tour told us yesterday."

At Forbes Island they ordered drinks and went to the edge of one of the sand patios. Behind them the heavy leaves from one of the palm trees made a scratching noise. He couldn't tell if the tree was real or just a very good replica. They watched the fog. Ferryboats made their way back to the city from Angel Island and Alcatraz. In the far distance, he counted at least a dozen sailboats. Melanie touched his shoulder.

Because he was too polite to come up with a reasonable excuse not to stretch a glass of wine into a meal, they ate together in the subaquatic dining room. He watched the green water outside the window above their table and tried not to think about being submerged. His wife, he thought, would love it here. She enjoyed unusual places like this. He knew exactly what she would tell her friends about the restaurant. "Only in America," she'd say. "A floating island! Can you imagine?"

Melanie was divorced. She and her daughter had been

visiting colleges in San Francisco, where her daughter wanted to go to school. This was their last day in the Bay Area. She wasn't really from Salinas, but it was the first city that came to mind when the tour guide asked.

During the meal, she asked if the bar at his hotel was nice. She asked what the view was like from his room. She leaned close to him across the table, mirroring his arm movements. She told him she was lonely. He understood what she was doing. To each of her questions, he answered honestly and briefly. He told her about his job, about his trip to California so far, though he was careful to leave out San Luis Obispo altogether. He also did not tell her he was married. He told her about how in middle school he'd lost the tip of his left index finger to frostbite. His class had been orienteering and he'd missed one of the control points near the end of the course and wandered into the thick forest until he'd reached a farmhouse about five kilometers from the orienteering course. He thought the story spoke to his carelessness, so he rarely told it. But at Forbes Island, he felt it might somehow dissuade Melanie from her pursuit. She asked to see his finger, and he showed her. She took it between two of her fingers and squeezed. Then she turned her head side to side, examining the stub from every angle. He watched her do this. There was really nothing remarkable about the missing finger. It looked like a normal finger, only a little shorter and missing a fingernail.

"Do you have phantom limb syndrome?" Melanie asked.

He said he'd never felt anything like that, and it wasn't an expression he'd heard in English, but he knew what she meant. He pulled his hand from hers. When it came, Martin paid the bill, although she offered to help.

"It's unseasonably warm," she told him outside. "The weather report this morning on the news said so. *Unseasonably warm* is a strange expression, don't you think? It's summer. It's supposed to be warm."

"Summer is often cold here," he said, repeating something he'd heard from one of the bartenders at his hotel just the night before. Whenever he was aware he'd done so, he felt embarrassed to correct women this way. They crossed the Embarcadero and walked several blocks into North Beach, finally catching a cab on Columbus not far from Washington Square Park, which Melanie pointed out as they passed. "You know your way around," Martin said. Melanie shifted nervously when he said this. She looked embarrassed, but he didn't know English well enough to know why. At the hotel, she suggested they have a nightcap. "Something for the road," she said. "Unless?"

He led Melanie into the bar, where they found a table near the television. The Giants, she explained while turning the pages of the cocktail menu, were playing the Dodgers. "It's a great rivalry."

After they'd ordered something to drink, he excused himself to use the restroom. He left the bar and entered the lobby, where he turned and looked back at Melanie. The drinks arrived while he was watching. Melanie sipped her drink through a straw and watched the baseball game. She clapped quietly when one of the Giants hit the ball deep into the outfield, and Martin wanted nothing more than to go home.

He took the elevator back to his floor and entered his room and locked the door behind him. He didn't answer the phone when it rang, and he didn't go to the door when someone knocked on it. He lay on the bed in the dark room and waited until he fell asleep. In the morning, he again checked out early and drove back to Los Angeles, where he stayed, uneventfully, for the rest of his trip.

The waitress at the Sakura Karaoke Bar brought another round of sake and Chinese beer. She knocked before entering. The room was warm and when the thick glass door opened, cold air rushed in and Martin felt this on his face. He was holding the microphone, waiting for the song to start. The waitress set the bottles on the table, gave a shallow bow, and backed out of the room. One of his colleagues pressed the play button on the console below the television. "Hotel California" began to play over the tinny speakers. Martin sang along for the first few bars. But soon he found himself thinking of Cesar in bed in San Luis Obispo. He saw the dark motel room, and through the opening in the curtains the black of the sky. Outside, a lamp mounted on the wall just above the large window cast an orange light back into the room, over Cesar and around him, and he moved side to side to music Martin could not now recall.

The Right-Hand Traffic Diversion

He tried again to explain it to his wife. Using first his hands, one fisted into a globe, the first finger on his other circling an exaggerated wobble, and then a crude sketch on the back page of the sports section of *DN,* he illustrated the inclination of the earth's axis. Agncta shook her head, said, "We're moving into darker days." His wife's figurative thinking often frustrated him. It was early, just ten after four in the morning. They were up to witness the right-hand traffic diversion. He had been waiting for months through the slow buildup of changes across the city. New street signs, bus stops. A new fleet of trams with doors on both sides. The measure to switch the flow of traffic from the left-hand to the right-hand side of the road had passed narrowly through parliament. Despite a widespread public education initiative and an aggressive advertising campaign, including songs and humorous sketches on state television and a line of women's underwear with the date September 3, 1967, printed across the seat, the change remained unpopular. But it was one he supported.

He refilled his coffee cup. "We'll lose a minute or two a day as we get closer to the equinox."

"I prefer the winter to the summer," his wife said. "In winter, we're on the way to better things. Summer is so unhopeful."

They had been discussing what time the sun would rise. The days were still weighted toward daylight, but he agreed with his wife that there was a dread to moving into the winter that was far greater than the hope of coming out of it. When they'd finished their breakfast, he cleared the table while Agneta finished dressing. He listened to the sounds from the bedroom—the sticky dresser drawer, the rattle of the hangers. By four thirty, he was holding the heavy front door of their building open for his wife.

The walk to Kungsgatan was not long. All traffic in the city had been stopped, so there were no taxis running. He liked the crisp late-summer air and the quiet. To prepare for the change, the traffic authority had installed new signs, painted new lines on the roads, erected new bus and tram stops. All of it was covered with black plastic, and as they walked he watched workers beginning the process of removing this plastic from the new and placing more plastic over the old.

As they got close to Kungsgatan, a crowd began to form, seeping off of small side streets like the headwaters of a river. When they'd turned onto Kungsgatan and passed the first shallow bend in the road, he saw this river of people interrupted by islands of yellow-vested traffic volunteers and police cars. Whistles blew, people shouted, and beneath those noises there was a sturdy hum of conversation from the crowd.

Agneta clutched his arm tight. They found a spot near the Astoria Cinema from which it was possible to see the middle section of the long line of police and military vehicles in the street. The cinema's sign reached high above them and glowed brightly, illuminating a rough circle of white light on the pavement at their feet. He pulled Agneta close.

At precisely ten minutes to five, a bell sounded. The crowd turned their faces to the still-dark sky. A hiss of static filled the air. The wide mouth of the loudspeaker mounted to the eaves of the building across the street gaped downward. It hissed again. "Now is the time to change over," a voice announced. The crowd applauded. He felt his wife's hand drop from his arm as they joined in the applause. People pushed from every side. He smelled them, felt breath on his neck and cheeks. As he pushed forward, he turned to look for Agneta. His glance settled on her hat, the sharp lines of her coat that she had insisted on wearing though it was, he had reminded her that very morning, still calendar summer. The crowd listed forward into the street. Engines started. He stepped awkwardly off the curb, looked down at the street, puddles dark against a dark background. He turned to look for his wife again, put his arm into the air, called her name. But she was gone.

He stopped and stood against the flow of the crowd but the angry looks and bodies pushing into the street forced him away from where she had been standing. The announcement sounded twice more and was followed by another bell, this one higher pitched and steadier.

A whistle stabbed the cold air. Slowly, the cars on the

street began to edge forward, the crowd parting. The traffic volunteers waved their arms wildly. They pushed pedestrians out of the way. From the opposite side of the street, he waited for his wife.

The hoary snarl of engines revved too high rose up from the street. It was still dark. The traffic moved slowly from the left lane to the right. Soon another signal sounded and the cars all stopped. The cars in the street directly in front of him now pointed east, toward a suggestion of dawn clawing up the valleys between buildings. His wife was missing. Shadows passed in front of headlights and each shadow did not belong to Agneta. Exhaust steam blossomed from behind each of the cars like a fog from a thawing pond.

At precisely five o'clock, the bell sounded once more. The change was completed and traffic was free to move. Several police officers joined the volunteers in the street. The police signaled at cars, the volunteers at pedestrians. It was over. The traffic diversion was completed, a part of history that could not ever be erased, and he felt, for a moment, angry with his wife for separating herself from him.

Every woman he saw was Agneta, every man himself. She disappeared around a corner, brushed against him as she passed. Her scent, the roughness of her coat, the softness of her hands against his. The city was suggesting her to him but did not offer her up. He searched up and down the street but the faces were indistinguishable from one another. Thousands of the same person, a swarm, surrounded him. He was being swallowed by the cold.

He walked quickly home, concentrated on the grinding of his shoes against the pavement. Straight ahead, less than a block from their building, he saw a woman. She was walking fast. He ran to catch her and as he approached he saw that her coat was all wrong, the shoes the wrong color, her hair not quite right. The woman stepped to one side as he ran past. "Agneta!" he called out.

In the courtyard, he looked up at his building. His own kitchen window was lit. His wife must have already arrived home. A fresh pot of coffee would be waiting, the day's newspaper, delayed by the traffic diversion, would no doubt be unfolded and waiting for him on the dining table. He felt himself flush with embarrassment as the panic left him. A radio played faintly.

Light bled out from beneath the front door of his apartment. He had been careful to shut the lights off when they had left. He was always careful to shut off lights, lock doors. He disliked wastefulness, positioned as much of his life as he could against theft and danger. Here was more evidence, proof, that Agneta had arrived home before he had.

He took his shoes off in the entryway, hung his coat. "Hello," he said. He calmed his voice, breathed deep, even breaths. "You got here first," he said. "Agneta?"

In response, he heard only the radio. They had not been listening to the radio at breakfast. Agneta disliked it during meals and he allowed her this though he preferred the news to conversation. It had hardly been an hour since he had been sitting at the table with Agneta. His diagram of the earth was still there, its rotation frozen. Tomorrow the sun would rise a minute later. The world rushed forward in spite of itself.

"Agneta?" he said again. He checked the bedroom, the guest room. He opened all of the doors. Their bed was made, her toiletries neatly replaced in the bathroom. A coat, not unlike the one she had worn that morning, hung stiffly on the dark cherrywood chair she liked to face the east-facing window. He checked the chair though he could see even from behind that she was not in it.

Agneta was not in the apartment, or if she were she was hiding from him, playing a cruel trick the reason for which he could not recall or perhaps had not ever known. Her absence meant something to him but he did not know what. The radio grew louder with every room he searched and every room that was empty.

In the window opposite the kitchen, he watched the sky lose its color. He walked toward this, into the darkened living room, and stood at the window. The sun reflected brighter and brighter in the windows of the building across the courtyard. Color returned to the sky as if it had been exhaled onto it. Each of the windows lit up sharply, a wall of white glass and yellow stucco. Daylight filled the room around him. He squinted his eyes against the light and saw only shapes. The shapes were unfamiliar, both too large and too small. He turned and moved away from the window, toward the dark opening of what he hoped was a door. A piece of furniture, a couch or the edge of a table, brushed against his leg. He reached out his hands, lurched forward, and felt no evidence of what he knew had once existed behind him.

To God Belongs What He Has Taken

Marie buys her morning coffee at the convenience store on the corner of her block. One of the men who works there is named Ahmed. He is Iraqi. When he laughs, which he does often, his enormous belly shakes. She likes Ahmed. She's been buying her coffee from him since she's lived on this block, almost two years. In a week, the sale on her apartment, her first, will be final and she and her daughter Tove will move in with Lennart. Marie has been marking this change by counting down the days until she will no longer buy her coffee from Ahmed's store. Lennart's grandfather died two weeks ago and Lennart inherited the big apartment on Kungsholmen. There was room for all of them. Sometimes Lennart says he wants children of his own, but Marie isn't sure she wants to go through raising another child. Counting the years she was traveling and Lennart was abroad with work and they were not together, she and Lennart have been in love, more or less, for fifteen years.

It's a very cold Monday in April. She goes to the store to buy her coffee on her way to work. She purposefully avoids the pastries aligned in neat rows in a glass case near the register. Her hands are cold and her fingers ache. She wraps her hands around the warm cup.

There is a new man behind the counter, whom she has never seen before. This new man is not as old, nor is he as fat, as Ahmed. He does not have the same kind eyes or funny, toothy smile. "Where is Ahmed?" she asks the new man.

"You haven't heard," he says.

"No," she says.

"Ahmed died on Saturday," he says. "To God belongs what he has taken." He points to his chest. "Heart attack."

Marie touches her fingertips to her throat. "Oh no," she says. "I'm so sorry." Just above the man's left nipple, the outline of which she can see very clearly beneath his shiny red shirt, he is wearing a name tag that reads, Ahmed. Below that, the name of the store curls in tight embroidered circles. This must be Ahmed's son, she thinks. "Were you," she says, "I mean, are you related to him? I'm so sorry," she says before he can answer.

"No no no," the new Ahmed says. "I only work here." He smiles. Marie smiles back. Then the man turns serious. "He appreciated all his customers," he says. It's a strange thing to say and the way he says it sounds rehearsed and stiff.

"I liked him too," Marie says. She tries to pay for her coffee but Ahmed puts his hands, palm down, on the counter. "A thank you," he says. The doorbell jingles and a new customer enters the store. It's another regular, a woman Marie recognizes. Marie is struck by a sentimental jolt. He's dead, she nearly says, nearly takes the woman by the arm. He's gone. It's the sort of tidy, packaged emotion one sees on television or in films, nothing more than a suggestion of real emotion. The feeling darts through her and passes quickly.

Marie sees the woman daily at the store. And they often take the same train into the city. The woman gets off one stop before Marie, at Odenplan. She's never talked to the woman, though once they sat across from each other on the metro and shared a smile when a young man sitting next to Marie said loudly into his telephone in a voice almost spilling over into a sob, "I don't want to fuck you and forget about you either!" Marie also sees the woman some evenings at the park near the shopping center, where the woman often comes with a dog, a large one, a Great Dane, Marie thinks, that trots along obediently behind the woman. She has seen the woman buying cards and flowers at the florist in the square close to the metro station. She's never seen the woman with a man, nor another woman for that matter, but she has seen the woman arm in arm with a much older woman at the pharmacist, at Systembolaget, at the post office, once at the supermarket. Marie has imagined a life for the woman, of course. Aging mother, no children, good job, civil servant perhaps. She travels frequently to places Marie has always wanted to visit, countries that are warm in winter—Chile, Vietnam, or Papua New Guinea.

She is standing in the way of a third customer, who, she sees as she follows Ahmed's gentle nod, is trying to pay for a bottle of water. "Excuse me," this third customer says. "Sorry," he says and pushes, politely, past Marie to the counter.

Perhaps they even look alike, this woman and Marie. Marie watches the woman at the coffee station. The woman turns to retrieve the milk from the cooler. In profile, they are different. The woman is far more delicate-faced than Marie is. She is taller, broader across the shoulders, but even in the coat she is wearing, obviously thin. Thinner than Marie. The woman is pretty and in spite of herself, Marie feels a little embarrassed to compare herself to the woman.

The third customer takes his change from Ahmed. He stiffly places the bills in his wallet and the coins in the coin pocket on the front of his wallet. By the time he has finished this, the woman has approached the register to pay for her coffee. The train Marie has planned to take leaves in ten minutes. It's an easy walk to the station and she prefers to wait here, where she can shorten her time spent in the cold. The outdoor platform is raised, and the wind, directed by rows of tall apartment blocks on either side, whips and stings its way from one end of the platform to the other. Marie moves close to the door but does not leave. Outside, there is still ice and a thin dusting of snow in the shadows. She's going to miss this neighborhood. It has been good to her and to her daughter. Her father thinks she's making a poor decision moving in with Lennart. She's crazy to sell her place and get out of the real estate market. Every time they speak he tells her this. Reinvest whatever money you make on the sale in a new apartment. Otherwise the taxes will wipe out whatever profits you may have made. It's silly to work so hard for something and then give it up just like that. He often frames his concerns for her personal life in economic terms. In truth, she appreciates his advice, though she tells him, as often as he offers it, that she is old enough to make her own decisions.

This is what she is supposed to say and so it is what she says, though she wishes she more often did what she wanted rather than what was expected.

Marie hears the woman say, "I'm sorry to hear that. Ahmed was a sweet man."

"He appreciated all of his customers," Ahmed says, and as he did with Marie, refuses to take the woman's money.

As the woman passes Marie, they share a crisp smile.

Marie steps out into the bitterly cold morning after the woman. It's a bright clear day, a winter day even though it is already spring. Marie slows her pace to follow the woman. There is a fast-moving line at the turnstile and they arrive at the same. Marie indicates with a hand that the woman should go ahead. On the platform, the woman retrieves a *Metro* newspaper from the vending machine, and continues down the platform until she stops near the midpoint. It's crowded here in the mornings, at the middle of the train, and not ordinarily where Marie waits for the train. Today she does. The woman unfolds the paper and begins to read. The paper shakes in the wind, the top of the pages folding over her hand. She tries to snap it back into shape but finally gives up and tucks the paper tightly between two slats on a wooden bench.

"That was very tragic," Marie says, surprising herself. She wants to introduce herself to the woman, lay bare the wonder between them, the way their lives have orbited so closely for so long; and now, tragically, but not overwhelmingly so, they have met here at the occasion of the death of such a kind man. This is something they share. She wants to talk with the woman, ask about what sort of life, if any, the woman might have imagined for her. Would the woman have conjured up Lennart, or Tove? By some indefinable ability to see patterns and cause and reason where there may be none, would she have guessed at any of the details of Marie's life? How much of another's life can we rightly assume when we see it only in passing bursts?

The woman looks at Marie and it occurs to Marie that the woman does not know that Marie has also been told about Ahmed's death, and also that she may assume that Marie was referring to the newspaper and the wind and the paper's current place on the wooden bench. "I'm sorry?" the woman says.

"Ahmed," Marie says, "the man who owns the shop. He died."

"Right," the woman says. Marie feels her disappointment in the woman's lack of sadness plainly in her chest. It's a hollow feeling, not physical exactly, but tightly woven inside her body. "I was sorry to hear that. Do you know how he died?"

Marie hesitates, brightens at the opportunity of the woman's question. "Heart attack," she says a little too hopefully, and takes a step closer to the woman.

"That's terrible," the woman says. "He can't have been very old."

"To God belongs what he has taken," says Marie.

"I suppose," says the woman, blinking. "I guess I don't know what that means."

Marie picks up the woman's newspaper and puts it in her purse. She does this loudly, deliberately. The woman looks at her. "I've seen you," Marie says. She feels her face flush with embarrassment but cannot control herself.

"I beg your pardon," the woman says.

"With your mother," Marie says. "I've seen you with your mother. That woman. Is that your mother?" Once, when Marie was a child, she pinched her sister as hard as she could until her sister began to cry.

The woman looks at Marie with a strange expression, turns her body to face Marie, and says, "My aunt, actually."

"She looks like you," Marie says. "Or you her, rather."

The woman stares at Marie. In the woman's face Marie can see as clearly as if the woman has spoken the words out loud that the woman is scared of her. Marie smiles at the woman and turns away from her. This is the polite thing to do, she thinks, the proper thing.

A man pushing a baby carriage is pacing back and forth along the platform. He has passed twice already. The baby is crying and the man is obviously nervous about this. He stops, not far from Marie, and puts a hand in the carriage, firmly rocking the baby side to side. "Shhhh," he says. "There's nothing wrong, be quiet." The baby is not crying loudly, and with the wind and the murmur of conversation and the static of the approaching train it is hardly possible to hear the baby at all.

Animals at Uneasy Rest

I

Thailand had become a little boring. He couldn't admit this to Jenny. She loved the heat. She loved the little bungalow they'd rented. She loved all of it and insisted, every year, that they come to Thailand in July, the worst month, Jacob was certain, to visit such places. The bungalow was cramped with musty air whenever the tall wooden slat blinds were closed, which is how his daughters liked it and so how it was, and Jacob's allergies had been acting up for the past few days. They'd been there a week, had a week to go, and Jacob hadn't slept well yet. He and Jenny had to share the bedroom with the girls. He resented this for two reasons in particular. One, he and Jenny hadn't had sex as much as he would have liked nor as much as he'd expected. Early in the trip they'd tried in the shower, when the girls were on the beach, and Jenny strained a muscle in her back and had to stay in bed for an entire day. Two, he snored. The girls made fun of him for this and their teasing hurt his feelings. It shouldn't have but it did. He tried hard to laugh with his daughters when they laughed at him every morning, pushed close up against one another with their breakfast at the little unstable dining table, but he couldn't. It hurt him.

One morning, fresh cup of coffee in his hand, Jacob was sitting in the rickety folding chair, which he had moved close to the sliding glass door overlooking the patio and little swatch of beach, when a koel landed on the patio railing. The sun reflected brightly off the white sand. The koel was a pretty bird, brown with white spots and bright crimson eyes. There was a storm coming in. He watched the clouds gather tall and dark out over the water. He'd read about the birds in a book on native flora and fauna. There weren't many books in English, and none in Swedish, on the bungalow's shelves. He'd read in the book that the koel was loud during mating season, March through August. The females produced shrill calls the book described as distinctive and spectacular. The bird stayed on the railing for eleven minutes. He timed it. He watched the waves and the bird and listened for its call, hoping to hear a sound he'd never experienced, but the bird just flew off.

After one afternoon of rain, they'd had sun for the rest of the stay. On the last day, he stood out on the beach, watching the waves punch the sand in uneven sets. Jenny and the girls were inside packing. They were waiting for the taxi to take them to the ferry that would take them back to the mainland and the airport. The sun had just come up and already it was hot. He listened to the waves, rubbed his hands over his arms, and felt the salt. It was beautiful, but he was done with it.

In Dubai, on the long layover, Kristina, their eleven-year-old, tripped and fell on the tile floor near the arrival gate. She bruised her knee severely and Jacob held her in his lap for over an hour as she cried. At first she cried deep, racking sobs that caused passersby to smile sympathetically, then short choppy intakes of breath that were barely audible. By the time they'd reached Arlanda, they were tired and sore and, though it was raining and he had to be at his office in fewer than eight hours, Jacob was relieved to be home.

II

Summer was when it really started. At the end of July, just after they'd come back from Thailand, Jenny was on her way home from a fiftieth birthday party Jacob hadn't attended. It was late and the freeway was empty apart from the trucks speeding north out to the islands and coastal towns. From a long way off, she saw the faint wash of headlights shining up and out onto the road. As she got closer, she saw that a car had overturned in the shallow ditch beside the road. She put her hazard lights on and pulled as far onto the shoulder as she could get without driving her car into the ditch. She called for an ambulance. It was a chilly night. As quickly as she could, she made her way down the gravel embankment. The driver, whose name she would later learn was Henrik Brandt, had been badly injured. There were no passengers. Henrik was buckled to the driver's seat. His hair brushed against the center ceiling lamp. The bones of his left arm had broken clean through the skin. They were chalky white and moist with blood. She felt her stomach turn. Saliva filled her mouth and she retched. The food from the party, the single glass of wine she'd allowed herself. She sat on the cold gravel beside the car and talked through the broken windshield. A radio program on North Korea had been playing when she came across the accident. She told Henrik about the program. He went in and out of consciousness as she spoke. The car was positioned toward the road and the headlights shone upward, over the lip of the ditch and out onto the road. Dust particles were charged static in the light. She told him about the birthday party she'd come from. It was for her friend Pernilla, whom very few people liked. She told him about Thailand and the bungalow they rented there every summer. It was on a beautiful island, the name of which she'd only just learned to pronounce properly. She told him she was having a difficult time trying not to be disappointed by the cool weather at home. She told him she liked ordering curry dishes so spicy she could not eat them. Beyond the car, a tall chain-link fence stretched left and right as far as she could see, parallel to the road. A leafy forest of birch shuddered at the fence line. She heard something in the forest and looked toward the noise in time to see the two glowing circles of a deer's eyes disappear into the darkness. She heard the sirens of the ambulance and saw faintly the flashing red and blue lights coming north from the city. The sirens approached and she went up to the road to meet them. She stood on the shoulder, looking down at Henrik's car as the paramedics examined him. They cut him loose from the seat belt and put him on a stretcher and placed him in the ambulance. Immediately, the ambulance rushed away. Jenny got in her car and waited. She sat and watched the tow-truck drivers, who had arrived not long after the ambulance departed, lift Henrik's car out of the ditch with a crane and load it on a flatbed truck. Then a policeman told her to go home, and she did.

He was watching a rebroadcast of a Liverpool versus Arsenal match that was playing on one of the sport channels. If it spoke to his completeness as a soccer fan or some abiding desperation in his character that he could remember watching the match on television when it first aired, he didn't know. May 26, 1989. He was nineteen and had just graduated from high school. He'd first watched the match in a bar on Kungsholmen. Jacob had been a Liverpool supporter his whole life, just like his father. He didn't have to watch to the end to know that Michael Thomas would score a goal late in injury time to win the match 2–0 for Arsenal. He'd cried in that bar, not big sobbing tears or anything, but he'd gotten misty eyed.

Regulation time had just ended when he saw the headlights of Jenny's car fill the narrow driveway. He was a little annoyed that she was home. The time alone was nice and he'd enjoyed the match. Quickly, he shut the television off and snuck upstairs. He didn't want to hear about the birthday party. Pernilla was annoying and snobbish. Whenever

Jenny spent time with Pernilla, she needed a good forty minutes to decompress, recount the entirety of Pernilla's offenses. Jacob slipped out of his jeans and pulled on his pajamas without turning on the light in the bedroom. He heard the front door open and close. He heard his wife on the stairs, and he shut his eyes and tried to breath evenly. The bedroom door opened. "Jacob," Jenny said. He didn't respond. He listened to her cross the room, her bare feet sticky on the hardwood floor. The light in the bathroom switched on. He listened to the water running, the loud flush of the toilet, more water running. The bathroom light switched off. He didn't open his eyes. Jenny sat on his side of he bed, ran her fingers through the back of his hair. "I saw something tonight," she said.

He knew if he lay still long enough, she would stop. He tried hard but after what might have been a minute or maybe a little bit more, he turned to her, blinked his eyes in a way that he thought would indicate that she'd woken him, and said, "You're home. How was it?"

"I saw something tonight," she said.

"At the party?" Jacob said.

"On my way home," she said. "An accident. It was awful."

Jacob propped himself up on his elbow. "You were in an accident? Are you all right?"

"Not me," she said. "A man. I sat with him. He was hurt. There was so much blood." Before she could finish, she lay down in the bed beside him and sobbed. Jacob wrapped his arm around his wife and held her without saying anything. He listened to her cry and felt his own heartbeat in his arm as he held her tightly. After a long time, she fell asleep, and Jacob took one of the blankets from the chair on Jenny's side of the room and draped it over her shoulder. It was late. He was hot and sat on the edge of the bed, as still as he could, and removed the socks he'd forgotten to take off earlier, trying as hard as he could not to wake her.

III

Not long after the accident, in the last week of July, maybe the first week of August, Jacob couldn't remember exactly which, Jenny started visiting Henrik in the hospital. The bruise on Kristina's knee had faded to a funny yellow color, and she'd nearly stopped limping. At first, he didn't believe Jenny when she told him she was visiting Henrik. It seemed so unlike her. There must be some other explanation. She wasn't the type to have an affair. He probably was, though the occasion hadn't presented itself.

One morning after his run he checked the GPS in her car. The route he found saved in the device led directly from their house to St. Göran's Hospital, where the glowing purple line extinguished in the parking garage. Over coffee that night after dinner, he told Jenny he knew she visited Henrik.

"Of course you do," she said. "I always tell you when I go." It bothered him that she didn't try to hide it. He would have tried to hide something like this. When he thought this, he understood that his wife was a better person than he was and this bothered him too.

He looked down at his coffee cup. It was nearly empty and the end of the coffee was translucent. He pushed the cup away. "What do you do when you visit?" he asked. One of the girls' cats had nuzzled itself up against his chair. He felt the easy rise and fall of its chest against his leg.

"I sit with him," she said. "I know it's strange, but I want to be there. I feel like I owe it to him."

He turned a sugar spoon so that its bowl was pointing toward his wife. For the past three days, he'd felt a sharp ache in his chest, just below where he thought his heart was located. He felt the pain now. It was a fist slowly clenching. He closed his eyes. This pain had been keeping him awake at night. This wasn't because he felt the pain with any regularity but because even when it wasn't present, he was sure it indicated some serious health issue and he was terrified to have it examined. He put his hand to his chest and began to knead at his soft, aging body. When he saw Jenny's glance move to focus on his hand on his chest, he began to scratch as if he simply had an itch.

IV

Near the end of August, he went on a weekend vacation to golf with his friends Edvin and Joel. He hated golf. It was a stupid and boring sport. On the second night of the trip, at dinner in a little Indian restaurant Edvin had suggested, Jacob told his friends about Jenny and her visits to Henrik.

Henrik had come between them. That was how he explained it. Edvin sipped from his drink, nodded along with all Jacob said. Joel kept his eyes on the television above the bar. A soccer match was on. Of course, it wasn't true that Henrik was the problem. That was the easy answer. Henrik was a symbol for something else. The more complicated answer was that Jacob himself had come between Jacob and Jenny. He knew that it was unfair for him to be angry with his wife.

She'd witnessed a terrible accident and felt linked, intractably, with the victim of that accident. He didn't understand it exactly, but none of it was unreasonable. That he was angry, on the other hand, was completely unreasonable. And it was because he understood this—because he wanted to allow his wife this simple thing and could not—that he was afflicted. This was a word he'd been using privately for roughly a week and knew was far past the appropriate register for whatever his problem exactly was. When Edvin pressed him on the issue, Jacob took a piece of ice from his drink with his fingers, put it in his mouth, and said, "She's being unfaithful to me." They'd long since finished the meal, plates cleared, a second then third round of drinks ordered.

Edvin was the head of the human resources department at a very large corporation and for this reason often gave unsolicited psychological advice. "If you're upset about Jenny visiting this man," he said, "you should visit too. Face your fear."

Just after this the soccer match that had been playing silently ended in victory for the Swedish side against a team Jacob thought might have been Latvia, and all around them applause erupted and the conversation was lost. Later that night, though, when Joel was in the bathroom and they were all quite drunk, Edvin put his arm around Jacob's shoulder and said, "I'm serious, Jacke. Visit."

The course was beautiful. Skirting the fairway along the sixth hole, the lake rippled with a light wind. He watched a heron land on the water. The bird nimbly waded into the tall grass at the shore to observe the golfers. Jacob regretted having told Joel and Edvin about his wife and Henrik. His left arm was numb and he thought, when he'd first woken up, hungover and sweaty, that it was because he'd slept funny on it. But as the morning progressed, the numbness had not gone away but only moved up his arm to his shoulder, and he started to worry that the pain in his arm was an early sign of a heart attack or stroke. He was young for both, of course, but Leif, a friend he, Edvin, and Joel all shared, had died the year before. A heart attack at the Friskis and Svettis gym at Hornstull. He was only forty-three. None of this would ever be resolved. If it wasn't Jenny and Henrik, it was his health, or his children, or improvements to his house. There was no shortage of things to worry about. It infected everything in his life, a counterweight to all that was pleasurable.

He was out. Edvin had just shot, placing the ball wide of the green on a narrow thumb of rough that hugged the lake. Jacob lined up for his shot, swung, and watched his ball land short, bounce high twice, and then skip onto the green, rolling to a stop just left of the pin. Edvin raised his club above his head, shouted, "Jacke!" The heron took off and for one very calm moment, Jacob didn't think about Henrik or Jenny or the shame of having admitted his fears to two friends he didn't particularly care for, and even when he focused his thoughts directly on it, he could not feel anything unusual in his arm. He saw only the white bird flying low above the water and the light blue morning sky.

V

Halloween had suddenly become a thing. He held a piece of a fabric that would soon be transformed into a wizard's cape and tried to think of when Halloween had arrived. He set the itchy brown piece of cloth down beside him on the couch and picked up his drink. Halloween wasn't a holiday when he was a kid. It wasn't even a holiday when his daughters were younger. Not that he could remember anyway. Three years, four tops. His wife, his daughters, everyone lately was acting like Halloween had always just been there. And it hadn't. He took a sip of his drink. It was late and he was helping Jenny make costumes for the girls. They needed them for school. Alex was going to be a wizard from *Harry Potter* and Kristina was going as a ladybug or a butterfly or something. He couldn't quite tell what the mess of fabric next to his wife was going to transform into.

He picked up the cape, kneeled on the floor with the fabric spread out in front of him, and measured out a rectangle like Jenny had asked him to. "When did this happen?" he said, waving his glass over the fabric.

"Halloween?" she said. "I think it's nice."

"When we were kids we went to the cemetery to light candles. It meant something. How does this look?" He sat back on his heels and looked at Jenny.

"Maybe even a touch longer," she said. "All Saints' is a little morbid, don't you think? And the church part of it bothers me."

He'd never been the type to raise the Swedish flag or celebrate the King's Name Day or anything. He knew a couple of the old songs but he had no particular attachment to any of it. This was no culture battle, but Halloween seemed so fake. It was like trying to live in an American television program. It bothered him. "Doesn't it bother you?" he said.

"Why should it? The girls love it. Costumes, candy. All their friends dress up."

"It's stupid," he said.

"Sometimes, Jacob," she said.

"We don't have to do everything they want," he said. "It's our job to give them the experiences they need to have. I don't think I'm wrong."

She pushed the fabric into a pile on her lap. Without looking up at him, she said, "I can do the rest. I don't need your help." He felt his own anger hardening, pushing him further into a position he didn't particularly care to occupy. He got up and left before the fight could start.

VI

Jacob spent the afternoon online, looking up information about comas. A woman in Florida was in a coma for thirty-seven years. Her name was Elaine Esposito, a name he liked because it sounded strange when he said it out loud. If they ever bought a dog, he let himself think, even as he knew it was a terrible thing to think, Esposito would be a good name. Next he read about a man in Alabama who woke up from a coma after twenty years. Like Henrik, the man had been in a car accident.

Jacob's fears always manifested as physical pain. For six weeks in the summer, he'd been convinced his heart was failing. Then it was a sharp cramping pain in his stomach, just behind his belly button, that had him thinking ulcer, possibly cancer. A swollen lymph node in his neck brought him through the fall into early winter with thoughts of leukemia. None of it corresponded directly with Jenny's visits to Henrik, but Henrik had become a kind of physical pain for him, a throbbing reminder that something was wrong, something that he was too scared to check.

Outside, an early storm bore down on the house and Jacob felt warm and safe indoors. Jenny was at the hospital. She'd met Henrik's wife, Lisa, on one of her visits and they'd become close. Jenny often cooked Lisa meals, took her out for the evening or else shopping in town. To keep her mind off Henrik, Jenny said, though she never qualified this statement with an explanation about how, exactly, these things prevented Lisa from thinking of her husband. In any case, they were close and whenever Lisa was at the house, Jacob had strict orders from his wife not to bring up Henrik or the accident.

He watched the snow through the window. Henrik wouldn't wake up. The doctors had been clear about this. His brain was too damaged. It was going to be a difficult winter. The weather reports called for heavy snow every year, but this year Jacob had a feeling he should believe it. He set his computer on the crowded little table beside the couch where he'd been sitting for the past hour and got up to look out the window. By the height of the snow against the hedgerow along his front walk, he estimated how much had so far fallen. If the cold stayed, they would have snow for Christmas. The sun had set and the light on the walk had come on, turning the snow in the driveway and on a little less than half of his front lawn a sickly orange color.

That morning, he'd woken to an odd fluttering sensation in his stomach, one that seemed related to or suggested by his heart. Both his grandfathers had died of heart attacks, and he drank too much, that was for certain. Heart trouble wasn't out of the question, probably even likely, and his fear of this was almost always present, if only just as a whisper. But by breakfast the feeling had passed and he'd gone to work and was able to lose himself in the report he was filing for accounting, and by the afternoon he'd nearly forgotten about it.

Jenny had been gone for a little over an hour and would be gone, it was likely, for at least another.

He knew the way to the hospital but still he followed the GPS. The voice said, "In 900 meters turn left at the traffic circle." He did this. Within thirty minutes he was parked in the hospital's small garage, watching a maintenance worker throw salt on the pathway to the main entrance. He watched the man finish this work before he got out of the car. On the concrete pillar beside him someone had painted a small black swastika and the words *Keep Sweden Swedish*. He read this sentence several times. He didn't worry that Sweden was becoming less Swedish, but clearly some people feared that, and he knew fear caused people to act strangely. Jenny's car was in the lot, about a dozen spots up from where he'd parked. He considered saying something about the swastika to the maintenance worker as he passed on his way into the hospital, but decided against it at the last moment and instead simply nodded to the man. "Watch your step," the man said. His accent was thick and his voice was very deep. "I've only just shoveled here. It's probably still icy."

Jacob stepped carefully from one patch of melted ice to another. Because he hoped to make it clear that he heard and understood what the man had said in spite of the man's accent, Jacob smiled broadly and nodded quickly. That he felt somehow guilty about the graffiti in the parking garage was an emotion he sensed distinctly but didn't care to explore.

Inside, he sat in the only available chair in the cramped waiting area nearest the door. He knew his wife was upstairs. He checked his watch. She'd be down in a half hour. He had that long to figure out if he was going to go up and see her or if he was going to wait for her here. Cold air rushed in every

time the doors slid open. He didn't take his jacket off. There
was a television mounted to the wall opposite the door. It
was showing a news program at very low volume. A panel of
guests was discussing the algae they already predicted would
be a problem in the lakes that summer. It was only December, Jacob thought, and already everyone was anxious about
what summer might bring. On the floor directly across from
him sat a dog carrier. There was a sleeping dog inside, a small
dog, its still head lit by a square of light streaming in from
above. He decided to go to Jenny, and walked toward the elevators. When he passed the dog, it woke up suddenly and
stuck its wet muzzle out through the cage. He heard the claws
clicking on the hard plastic. The woman who owned the dog
smiled at Jacob and said, "He must like the way you smell."

He stood in front of the tall orange letter *n* on the wall
beside the row of elevator doors. The doors were polished to a
sterile glimmer. Jacob almost wanted to reach out and touch
one of them. There was a sandy beach in Grimsta where he
and Jenny liked to take the girls to swim when it was warm.
A long floating dock had been built out into the water and at
its end there was a slide. The beach was sometimes closed if
large amounts of algae had been detected in the water, and on
those days the slide and dock looked solemn and tragic bob-
bing up and down in the wind. Every year the algae made
people sick, usually children who drank the water. No one
had ever died as far as Jacob knew, and the beach closings always struck him as overly cautious and unnecessary. An elevator arrived with a ding. The doors opened to three people.
Jacob moved to get on the elevator and then stopped. One of
the people, a nurse in green scrubs, put her hand out to hold
the door. "I'll take the next one," Jacob said. He stared at the

three people and they stared back, smiling, until the doors closed.

Another elevator came and again he didn't get on it, though this one was empty. He thought about algae and lakes and the way his daughters used to fight over which of them would get to dress as Lucia in the St. Lucy's Day processions at their school. The girls were still young but they'd grown out of such arguments and into others, and he couldn't remember when or how that had happened. He thought about Henrik Brandt, upstairs with the television and with Jenny, and he thought about the immigrant worker outside in the cold, fighting endlessly against the snow and ice. He felt the fluttering make itself known in his stomach again and put a finger to his pulse to see if he could determine some connection. He stood this way in front of the elevator for a few minutes until a nurse, evidently finishing her day's work, stopped and, standing too close to him, asked if he felt unwell. He thanked her and went back outside and got in his car. Jenny's car was still up the row from his. The worker was gone but a fresh layer of sand had been laid over the path and he could still see a hint of yellow peeking through the wet snow. He started the car and turned on the heater. While the car warmed up, he rubbed his hands together and watched the snow. A woman left the hospital, holding a newspaper above her head—a hopeful but pointless gesture in such heavy snow—and he watched her cross to the parking garage. As she passed his car, he followed her with his gaze and his eye caught the swastika again. Over the summer, graffiti like this had started to appear on the glass walls of the bus stop Jacob used every morning. There were swastikas and the double letter *s* that looked like lightning bolts. The images appeared fresh every Monday when Jacob went to wait for his morning bus. For six weeks straight they were there. Once or twice the symbols had been etched into the glass, but normally they were written in thick black marker or spray paint. The graffiti was usually cleaned up by the middle of the week, but by the following Monday it was always back. Then a neighborhood boy was arrested for riding his motor scooter on a school playground and as suddenly as the graffiti had started appearing on the bus stop, it stopped. For a few days afterward, Jacob and Jenny and their neighbors seemed invigorated with the proof that they lived in a nice neighborhood, a welcoming and safe place, in which this kind of hatred was only ever a prank. He told himself he was going to go back into the hospital and tell the receptionist about the graffiti so that she would tell whoever was in charge of such things that the vandalism needed to be removed. He was so convinced that this was a thoughtful and generous act, and he thought it out in such detail that by the time he was pulling out of the parking garage and easing out into traffic he'd already forgotten what he'd planned to do.

VII

Sometime between using the toilet and getting up from it, his pants had arranged themselves in such a way that the zipper's pull tab had worked itself into the crease at the bottom of his fly. These were his favorite pants. First, he tugged at the pants, hoping the movement might cause the pull tab to dislodge itself. It didn't. He dug his finger into his fly, hoping to force it loose. Nothing. Then he pinched the slider, tried to zip it upward. It was difficult to get a good grip and it didn't budge. On the other side of the bathroom door, Jenny was packing for Copenhagen. Normally, Jenny would have fixed this sort of problem. She was capable and patient, but he didn't think he could ask for her help without starting another fight. It all made him sad. Lately, that was the only emotion he could feel. Never frustrated, rarely angry, but always sad. He reached down to his fly, determined to free the pull tab by pulling the flap of the fly outward with his left hand as he positioned his right index finger as far behind the pull tab as possible. Still it would not budge. The tip of his finger stung and was tender from the effort. A feeling that reminded him of claustrophobia began to settle in his shoulders and back. He felt warm, and turned on the faucet for a drink. He placed his mouth to the stream of water. The water tasted earthier than normal, as if it might be coming from deep underground.

For the past week Jenny had been trying to convince him of the economic benefits of geothermal heating. Her point, he recalled, gulping down a second mouthful of cold water, was that they were already paying thousands of kronor a month for heating and the geothermal system would, in her words, obliterate that cost. He pulled his mouth from the stream of water to take a breath. It would pay for itself in nine months. She'd read this in the materials that arrived in the mail. Nine months worked out to roughly two winters. The math was sound, no question. Still, there was an obstacle to his coming around to Jenny's side on the issue. The purchase and installation of the geothermal system were so costly they would need to make financial sacrifices. The new car would have to wait. Same for the four days in Åre they took every year during sports week in February with the girls. Same for their annual trip to Thailand. They always started saving for Thailand just after Christmas. He placed his lips back to the stream and drank two or three more gulps of cold water.

In the mirror, he picked at an ingrown hair on his neck. Maybe the geothermal heating system would offer an opportunity for long-term financial savings, plus the chance to stay at home for the whole month of July for once. If he agreed to have the system installed, he could call the installation company and request that they do the work in the month of July. He loved July in Stockholm. Everyone was on vacation. Patio service at his favorite bars stayed open late. They could rent a boat, maybe take it out and camp on an island or two in the archipelago. With a pair of Jenny's nail scissors he made a small incision at the base of the fly. This allowed him to pry the pull tab upward with his finger. He ran his fingernail the length of the incision. It was a simple thing, but they needed to remember the value they held for each other. This is what she said when she'd proposed the idea of taking a trip, just the two of them. He agreed. He dragged the zipper up and down a few times to check that it hadn't been damaged. It hadn't. He held the pants tightly against his chest.

Jenny's voice came through the door. "It's five to three. What are you doing in there?" He looked at his watch. The pants had cost him fifteen minutes. He left the bathroom for the bedroom, where Jenny was making neat piles of their clothing. The suitcase was halfway filled. She shook her head at him. "I hope you're not coming down with that bug Alex had last week."

He held the pants up. "Some trouble with my zipper," he said.

"Want me to take a look?" she asked.

"I'll bring a different pair," he said. He took a pair of jeans from his stack on the bed, pulled them on.

Jenny held up two socks. He sat on the corner of the bed and watched her tuck them into a ball. Outside it was snowing. It was three days into the new year.

"I say we go for it," he said.

"What?" she said.

"Geothermal," he said. "The heating. I think it's a good idea."

She folded a shirt. "That's a change," she said.

"I'll move some money around." He was trying hard to sound agreeable.

She put the shirt neatly in the suitcase, smoothed it. "If you think so," she said. He heard caution in her voice. Her sister had come to stay for the weekend. She was downstairs, watching television and making plans with the girls about what they would get up to for the weekend. Snow was forecast every day.

Jenny was smiling. She arranged a pair of heels upright at the hem of a green skirt. "Too summery, do you think?" she asked.

"Beautiful," he said. "I've always liked that skirt."

She smiled at him and placed her makeup bag carefully on top of Jacob's sweaters. The sweaters were bulky and though she pushed the bag down firmly it rose up above the lip of the suitcase when she removed her hand. She pushed again, this time with two hands. The bag still rose back up but she appeared to be satisfied with her efforts because she went to the closet and took out two of his ties, a black one with gray stripes and a solid red one. "I'm putting a choice of ties in here," she said, folding the ties together at their middle and laying them in the suitcase. "Pernilla was in Copenhagen last month and said there was an excellent restaurant in one of the hotels on the harbor. I can't remember which one. Remind me to call her when we land." Jacob nodded his head to all of this but wasn't listening.

She replaced the green skirt with something darker. "This is going to be good for us," she said. She smiled at him and moved the ties from atop the sweaters and tucked them into the little zipper pocket. She closed the pocket. "I think this will be fun, Jacob." He watched her hand reach over the suitcase and touch his shoulder. "The holidays," she said as if she was going to say more about it.

Her back was to him and he watched her bend over to pick up from the floor a pair of socks she'd decided not to take. His wife was a beautiful woman. Her hips were round and soft. Copenhagen would be good for them. He reached out and touched her. Without standing up, she turned and smiled at him. "That was nice," she said. "I'm looking forward to the trip, too. I miss you."

"Me too," he said.

In the long week between Christmas and New Year, Henrik Brandt had been taken off life support. Jenny spent the day leading up to this with Lisa at the hospital. Jacob had taken the girls out to ski on the trails in Grimsta. They'd had a big storm three days after Christmas and the snow was heavy but not too wet and the temperature was perfect for skiing. He'd enjoyed himself. The girls had gotten along with each other, and he'd had a good workout. They were almost old enough to keep up with him and he hadn't had to stop to wait as much as the previous winter.

He looked at his wife. She was holding a nightgown he liked. "I almost forgot," she said. He watched her fold it up into an impossibly small square and stuff it into the suitcase. "That's it," she said, "unless you've forgotten something."

"I don't think I have," he said.

VIII

Jacob picked up the suitcase and followed Jenny out of their bedroom. If they wanted to make it to Arlanda in time for their flight, especially with the snow, they had five minutes to say good-bye to the girls and get on the road. They walked down the stairs. Jacob balanced the suitcase against his hip. It was heavy and he grunted a little with the weight. "Are you sure you feel all right?" Jenny said. "You were in the bathroom a long time."

"I'm fine," he said.

Downstairs, Jenny went straight for the hall and pulled on her boots. In the small windows above the door, Jacob could see that the snow had picked up considerably. It was coming down hard. He saw Jenny see this too. She opened the door and it became instantly cold in the entryway. He watched the snow come down in a great pulsing wall. It was nice to look at. She said something to him. He didn't hear her but he sensed that she'd said something to him. He felt the weight of the suitcase in his hand and heard the sound of the television in the living room. She said, louder this time, "I said, What are we supposed to do now?" He set the suitcase down on the floor and looked at his wife. He listened to the girls laughing at a cartoon on the television. It was one he sometimes watched with them. He could almost picture the main character. It might have been a talking bear or some kind of large bird but as hard as he tried he could not remember.

The Winter War I

It was a week before Easter and snowing so hard Lennart had to tuck the bouquet of tulips inside his coat. The cold weight of the stems pushed against his chest. It was April the eighth, his grandfather Bent's ninetieth birthday. Lennart was on his way to his grandfather's apartment. To coincide with the arrival of spring, Moderna Museet was hosting the premiere of a piece of digital artwork called *The Winter War*. Bent was a surviving veteran of the actual Winter War, a fact upon which the Strand family had hung much pride for more than half a century. Bent rarely spoke of the war with his grandchildren, but as he got older it seemed to Lennart that Bent's memories of the war became fresher, more present. He would occasionally recount surprisingly detailed events from his time in Finland—the names of other soldiers, the results of a particular battle. There were more gruesome stories too. The sight of blood freezing solid the instant it fell to the snow from a neck torn open by gunfire. A leg severed by a mortar round, upright, boot still strapped to ski. When Lennart had seen the announcement for the premiere, he'd immediately invited Bent to attend. It was a birthday gift. He was the only one of his siblings who still visited their grandfather. Magnus and Ulrika lived abroad, and Matilda was always busy with her own family. Their father, Rolf, had died a year ago in June and since then Bent had become Lennart's responsibility. He'd been home from the United States just short of a year. His time there was so long ago, only a memory untethered to his life now. Since he'd been home he and Marie had been together again. They were in love in high school and hadn't seen each other in years. But in December, he'd run across her and her daughter, Tove, in front of the NK Christmas window displays. He'd gone, as he did every year when he was child, to see the spectacle, when he saw Marie in the crowd. She was standing in front of a home decor display, eyeing a low yellow table and a red Margrethe bowl full of silver apples. Tove stood with her face close to the fingerprinted glass of the window display. At first he didn't think it could be her, but as he passed, she turned, smiled at him, and said his name. It was snowing.

He chose not to believe in fate, but here they were only a few months later, the three of them a family. He supposed he should have been grateful for whatever coincidence had brought them together again, and he was, but he was also bothered by the pressures of the story. It felt scripted. The expectations he and Marie had, and those that were placed upon them by family and the mutual friends they still had, were unreasonably high. The chance meeting at the department store after all those years suggested an inevitability to the relationship that struck him as unfair.

After they'd graduated from school, they planned on attending Stockholm University together, where they both wanted to study biology and math and become schoolteachers. It was going to be a nice life, a comfortable one, and they both longed for it. But over that summer, Lennart was unexpectedly admitted to Chalmers University of Technology. The choice to attend was much easier than he'd anticipated. He studied engineering, got a job with Ericsson, and moved every couple years from one country to another. Sweden, then Morocco, then the United States, now back to Sweden. Of course, he and Marie lost touch during that time, but he also hadn't found anyone else. Neither had Marie. Tove's father was an Englishman named Ronnie whom Marie had met on a ski vacation in Austria. According to Marie, it was nothing serious and was over even before Tove was born. The whole thing felt arranged to Lennart, like it was being forced on him.

Bent's apartment building was pastel green and six stories high. The neighborhood was quieter than his and the apartment was much bigger. He and Marie had talked about moving in together, though not much, as she thought waiting for Bent's death was a little morbid. The apartment had plenty of room. Five bedrooms, an airy formal dining room used mainly as a library, a huge balcony with wrought iron railings. Lennart probably could take over the apartment even now, but Bent had refused to move into the assisted living facility and Lennart didn't press the issue. After a long bureaucratic battle with the municipal health administrators, Bent won the right to have a nurse come four days a week to help with necessities.

Lennart let himself in with his spare key. From the hallway he said, "Hello, hello!" and was sure to make enough noise that Bent would hear him. He hung his coat and unwrapped the plastic from the tulips and stuffed it into his coat pocket.

The television was on in the living room. A large frowning sun rushed from one side of the screen to the other. Then a drab meteorologist with a bald head and wispy ponytail called for snow on Easter Day. Lennart kissed his grandfather on the cheek. "Hello," he said again. The channel went to commercial. A normally expensive mattress shop was offering sharply reduced prices (up to 50 percent) on Jensen mattresses if it snowed on Easter. "It's a bold move," Lennart said.

"I suppose it is," Bent said. "One has to take risks now and again."

"Happy birthday, Grandpa."

"There's a war looming."

"I brought flowers," said Lennart, ignoring his grandfather. He'd had to learn to do this increasingly as his grandfather got older. "Tulips. I'll put them in a vase for you." He went to the kitchen and pulled a vase down from a shelf and filled it with cold water. "How are you today?" he called over his shoulder in the direction of the living room. He broke the stems off under running water and arranged the flowers in the vase.

"I'd like a beer," Bent said. His doctors recently forbade alcohol. Switching to beer was as close to obedience as Bent was willing to go. Lennart hadn't pressed the issue. Bent was ninety years old. Every week, Lennart restocked his grandfather's refrigerator. He took out two beers. There was a glass on the counter and he tucked this under his arm on his way out of the kitchen. Bent turned the volume on the television down and breathed loudly out of his nose. "Who are you again?"

"Your grandson," Lennart said and opened one of the beers, pouring half of it, too quickly, into the glass. "Lennart. I'm here to take you to the museum. *The Winter War,* remember?" Snow had accumulated on the balcony. Beyond this, he watched cars pulse across the bridge.

"I thought you were my nurse. He steals from me."

When the foamy head of the beer had settled, Lennart gave his grandfather the glass of beer and then sat down on the corner of the coffee table. "Do you want me to call the agency again?"

"Salim says he's from Tripoli," Bent said. "Is that a real place?"

"It's a city in Lebanon," Lennart said. "There's also a Tripoli in Libya."

"I thought I'd made it up," said Bent.

Lennart switched the television off. "It's a real place," he said. "Two real places."

"Anyway, I've never been there."

"You should wear a suit tonight," Lennart said. "Do you need help getting dressed?" He'd arranged an official invitation for his grandfather from the Arts Council on the grounds that Bent was a veteran. He had the invitation mailed to his grandfather's apartment, where he knew Salim would read it aloud. Every afternoon, Salim opened and sorted the mail according to its nature. Bills he stacked on the table in the hall for Lennart to collect and pay, which he did the twenty-seventh of every month from an account at Nordea Bank. He'd taken this task over from his father, and though he was not very good at managing his own finances, he always paid his grandfather's bills on time.

Bent pointed toward the dim hall. "Suit's in there," he said.

Lennart helped his grandfather undress. Then he knelt, held Bent's pants open and still as Bent sat on a kitchen chair and maneuvered each foot into each leg. Bent stood. Lennart fastened Bent's pants, helped him with his jacket. When Bent was dressed, Lennart helped him back to his chair. He turned the television back on, poured his grandfather a fresh beer, and lay on the couch to watch the snow.

At a quarter to seven, to the sounds of a loud and confusing television game show in which it appeared contestants were asked first to deny and then to reveal embarrassing personal information to a jeering audience, Lennart got ready to go. He tied his tie and put on his jacket. In the hall mirror, he watched himself flex his shoulders and cross his arms, trying to stretch the fabric of his suit coat so that it fit less snugly. He always gained weight in the winter and it hadn't come off yet. He settled for not buttoning the jacket. Then he called for a taxi.

The cab was idling in the street when they emerged from the entryway into the light snow. The apartment building was at the top of a short hill. Lennart was careful to hold his grandfather's elbow tightly. "Well," said Bent, "it's snowing."

"It is," Lennart said.

Bent looked up at the cloudy sky. "We're moving into lighter days," he said. Marie sometimes used these old-fashioned expressions.

"We should be in them already," Lennart said. "But I like the snow." The driver got out of the car and opened the front and back passenger doors. Lennart helped his grandfather into the back and fastened the seat belt. In the front seat, Lennart and the driver looked at each other, smiled hello.

The drive from Bent's apartment to Moderna Museet was short, but dull, and Lennart tried to persuade the driver to take a meandering route over two bridges and back up into the city from the south—he enjoyed the views of Stockholm from all but two of its bridges, especially in the snow—but the driver only chuckled at the recommendation and took Norr Mälarstrand instead. In no time, they'd arrived.

There was a red carpet leading up a pathway to the entrance of the museum. In a diffuse shadow behind one of the exterior lights, two men stood poised with brooms to sweep the collecting snow from the red carpet. A young woman in a black coat and white hat gestured toward the museum and said, in English, "Welcome to *The Winter War*." Lennart smiled. Inside, he and his grandfather shared a hanger in the coat check. The fee was sixty kronor. Lennart didn't leave a tip for the attendant. The lobby of the museum was lit much like it normally is—bright lights, shiny marble floor, stainless steel handles on tall pine doors. One of the doors was open. Lennart heard voices and music from out of the dark inside. He and Bent entered.

Men in shorts and tuxedo jackets roamed the room, serving drinks and offering appetizers. Lennart considered taking one but didn't. He recognized a television actor and one of the newsreaders from TV4, whose voice he'd always found attractive. A woman in a long white dress stood in a corner, offering a dramatic vocal performance in which she produced no sound. "This is unusual," Bent said. In the far corner, a group of people in all-white clothes danced beneath a black light.

Lennart led his grandfather into a room that was set up to resemble a theater. Rows of chairs faced a wall of thick curtains. White ribbons had been attached to the heating vents on the walls. In the warm air, the ribbons waved a pantomime of a winter storm. Lennart listened to the murmuring of conversations coming to an end and the clinking of glasses being placed on the floor. A glass or two toppled over. There was some distant laughter. The room was humid with late winter. Lennart helped his grandfather up the center aisle. They took seats near the front. Almost immediately, the room grew darker. The curtains parted to expose a projection screen and on the screen appeared the image of a summer cottage. It was a traditional Swedish summer cottage with white trim and Falu-red planks running vertical to the ground and a small garden surrounded by a short, white fence. The camera stayed fixed on this image.

Lennart saw light reflected on the screen from an opening door at the back of the theater. Then a man in a tuxedo walked in front of the screen and tapped a microphone pinned to his lapel. A faint light was directed at him from above. He introduced himself as the artist and thanked the audience for coming. The audience applauded. "The footage you're about to see has been manipulated, but much of it was first recorded during the Winter War and can be found in its original form in the national archives." He pointed at the screen. "The cottage you see behind me is my summer cottage in the archipelago, and the film comprises a single year, compressed into seventy-five minutes." There was more applause, and then the artist continued. "This is called *The Winter War*." He walked from the stage and sat down in the front row. The scene irritated Lennart and he crossed and uncrossed his legs twice.

Nothing appeared to be happening on the screen. Soon Lennart saw movement. Wind rustled the bare branches of two tall birches to the left of the cottage. A bird landed on one of the trees and immediately flew out of frame. It was night. Then it was day. This happened slowly at first and then very fast until he was unable to determine which was day and which was night. A single flower in the garden bloomed. Others soon followed. The grass up against the cottage grew long where it would have been difficult to trim. There were blurs of movement across the frame, the artist, he assumed, coming and going. Everything moved fast. Then, as suddenly as they'd bloomed, the flowers wilted and died. The leaves on the trees turned yellow and red and fell to the ground. It rained and then it cleared. The brightness of the sunlight shone out into the room, illuminating faces in the first two rows. Everything slowed down. A storm moved in above the cottage. It started raining again. The rain turned to snow. Snow covered the grass, the roof, the windowsills. The garden disappeared. There was only the white of the snow and the red of the cottage. Icicles reached for the ground from the rain gutters. The sky was gray.

In the foreground a group of soldiers appeared. They were crouched in a trench. He counted at least a dozen. They moved with unsteady motion about the trench. Beyond them the cottage loomed. The trench stretched the length of the bottom of the frame. The camera angle and contrast of the two scenes flattened the perspective, removed the image's depth. Lennart blinked against the light. The soldiers were dressed in white capes that blurred the falling snow against the dirt of the trench. Some of the soldiers stood and looked over the edge of the trench at the cottage and the violent storm engulfing it. Others faced the audience. Their rifles leaned against the dirt. Snow collected on heads. He watched the screen to see what was going to happen next. The sound of a distant plane grew louder. Soon the whistle of falling bombs filled the room, and there were several explosions in front of the cottage. The room lit up orange. People in the audience flinched. He heard the rustle of their clothes. Snow and dirt rained down on the soldiers, who all crouched low and covered their heads. Smoke hung thickly, obscuring the cottage and the soldiers. When it cleared, the cottage appeared to be undamaged. The soldiers stood, one by one, their backs to the audience, and rested their rifles on the lip of the trench, watching the cottage. This lasted so long that Lennart's left leg fell asleep. The opening door at the back of the theater opened wide rectangles of light on the screen several times as people streamed from the audience.

Slowly, the sky began to clear. It stopped snowing. Bright sun soon reflected off the snow. One of the soldiers removed the hood of his white cape and looked up at the sky. The snow began to melt from the roof of the cottage, large pieces of ice and snow falling into the garden. The soldiers continued to watch. The branches on the birch reached upward, and the snow kept melting. Soon the image of the soldiers faded and one by one they disappeared until the trench was empty. It too then disappeared. The snow was gone. The grass turned a deep green and flowers rose from the garden. Birds arrived to land on the branches of the birch trees, and on the warming rain gutters of the cottage. It rained for thirty seconds and was again clear. The blue sky above the house became very bright. The screen turned white and then gray. As the lights came on in the room and it emptied of guests, Bent turned to Lennart and said, in a strong clear voice that surprised Lennart, "I wonder if it happened like that."

Lennart helped his grandfather from his seat and offered him his arm. Together they walked into the main room. He led Bent to a group of red armchairs arranged in a neat circle near the bar. In the center of these chairs a low table held empty glasses. All around the group of chairs, people lingered. A man in a gray suit held one hand on the back of the chair nearest the bar. With the other hand, he turned a long-stemmed glass of wine in small tight circles in front of his chest as he spoke. Lennart helped Bent lower down onto a chair. The man glanced at Lennart and Bent and then at Lennart again, and moved his hand.

"Was it like that, do you think?" Bent said. A ring of water on the table broke its formation and crept slowly to the edge of the table.

"A version of it, I guess," said Lennart. "You were there."

They sat without saying much for a long time. Lennart ordered them drinks, then soon after a second for himself. When Bent finished his first beer, Lennart ordered them each another.

Behind Bent's head, a light was positioned in such a way that it shone directly around Bent's profile and onto the ceiling above the dance floor, alternating colors from red to green to blue and back. The film had bothered Lennart. It struck him as indulgent, its central metaphor somewhat foolish. Winter was long and difficult. Sweden had once fought in a war. The images were striking, beautiful even, but as a project the whole thing felt flat to him. He was particularly interested in asking his grandfather about death. It was the one thing the film managed to get right, although he'd been thinking about it since they sat down in the bar and had been unable to formulate a clear thought about how he might define this rightness. The drunker he got, the closer he got to collecting his thoughts into a recognizable shape. There was no death in the film, apart from the idea that winter itself represented, but there was something else. Something in the soldiers, their postures or the way they held their weapons and peeked, almost childlike, over the lip of the trench, managed to define their mortality, to suggest their fate without resorting to the blunt shorthand of violence. This was the one part of the film he'd enjoyed. It had rattled him. Lennart had experienced death. His father's, of course. And there was a friend in grammar school, Henning his name might have been, he couldn't remember, who died of cancer. A girl he liked when he was younger got so drunk at a party their first year of high school that she froze to death on a park bench in Vasaparken. A cousin drowned on vacation in Spain. Each of these deaths had, of course, likewise rattled him, but the film reached him more deeply.

Bent would die soon. He looked at his grandfather and thought this, very clearly, without emotion. The oncologist Bent visited last month had suggested Bent not choose to undergo chemotherapy. He'd been firm with his recommendation. Bent was old, the doctor explained to Lennart, and his body would probably not withstand the treatment. Lennart understood the doctor's position. It was one Bent agreed with in the taxi on the way home from the clinic, but still the idea of doing nothing bothered Lennart. Given the capabilities of modern medicine, why shouldn't Bent be kept alive as long as possible? But now, in the bar, drunk, he was struck by how simple the answer was.

"I don't think it was anything like that," Bent said. "It was slower. That winter was the longest winter I remember."

Lennart wasn't resistant to the idea of his grandfather being allowed to die because he wanted his grandfather to continue to live. Bent's death would come soon, Lennart knew that. But he hoped that his relationship with Marie would end before Bent died. It was a simple thing for him to understand and he was surprised it hadn't occurred to him before.

"I remember that cold gave us all sores on our legs," Bent said, and slowly reached a large knuckled hand up and down his thigh. "Can you imagine the pain?"

Lennart leaned toward his grandfather and spoke clearly but quietly so that Bent would be able to understand him but probably not hear what he said. "I'm going to end things with Marie, Grandpa."

Bent looked small in his chair. Lennart waited for a response from his grandfather, though he knew there wouldn't be one.

Shortly before eleven, he called a taxi.

Outside, the snow had picked up and a fresh layer coated the rolled-up red carpet. The taxi was waiting for them. Lennart didn't request a particular route home. He watched the headlights of passing cars. He leaned his head against the headrest and closed his eyes. They passed the Opera House. The building had been wrapped in a mesh wrap to cover renovation work that was being done. On the wrap was printed an old image of the Opera House. The wrap had been meticulously lined up with the building underneath, leaving only the peaks of the green copper roof that crowned the Opera

House visible. He'd read about the renovations in the paper. The image depicted the Opera House as it was in the late nineteenth century. Horses and carriages filled the plaza. People posed on the steps. The scale was too big, the people and all the objects unbelievably tall.

The snow was falling heavily, veined in all directions at once in the headlights of the taxi. The driver turned to Lennart. "I'll get you both home. Don't worry." They traveled slowly, but soon the taxi was turning onto Bent's street. The incline of the street rose sharply at the intersection. The plows wouldn't be out until the storm weakened. Snow fell hard from the orange clouds onto their shoulders as they shuffled from the curb to the building.

Upstairs, Lennart went from room to room, turning on lights. He set the thermostat. He helped his grandfather undress and get into pajamas. They drank another beer together at the kitchen table. It was probably just exhaustion but Lennart was drunk. He could pinpoint the feeling in his chest, a sleepy feeling that suggested both hope and fright.

Bent finished his beer and Lennart asked if he wanted another. "No," Bent said, placing his hand over his glass. "That film wasn't very good."

Lennart was surprised by his grandfather's lucidity, and looked closely at him as if to confirm that he'd heard correctly. "I guess not," he said.

"It was too fast," said Bent, placing his hands on the table in front of him and shaking his head. "It wasn't like that, everything speeded up. Just the opposite."

"No," Lennart said. "I suppose not." At one o'clock, he helped his grandfather into bed. When that was done, he typed a text message to Marie, though it was late and he hoped he wouldn't wake her. "Finished now," he wrote, just drunk enough to send the text without considering the double meaning. He was surprised when he got a response. "How was it?"

"It was fun," he typed. Then he deleted that and tried to think of a clever word for inauthentic, for fake, one he wouldn't have to explain to her in any great detail, but he couldn't focus and simply wrote, "Had a good time. See you tomorrow."

By four, the storm had passed. He went out on the balcony, the icy snow crunching under his feet. Below on the street, a siren, car horns, the horse-breath exhale of bus hydraulics. The sun crept upward and Lennart watched the city change colors.

The Apartment

Louise knew someone had moved in by the new name on the call box. She'd seen lights and movement in the apartment, which was across the courtyard from her and Martin, for the past few days. The new name confirmed it. Someone had finally bought the place. The name had been typed onto a small green piece of paper and taped to the call box beside the apartment's number. She'd known a man with the name Jahani at school. Arman had been a doctoral student in French the year she'd started at Stockholm University. He'd taught the conversation tutorial she took fall term. She looked at the green paper again. All that was so long ago. He was the second man she'd ever slept with. Martin still didn't know about it. She checked her watch. She was on her way out to meet her son Jonas for lunch. The metro she wanted to take was due in ten minutes. Arman had come from Iran to study, or maybe he'd come to escape the revolution. She couldn't recall the details now. The years fell into one another. A bus rushed past on the street and the blast of warm air stung her neck.

Jonas wanted to try a sushi restaurant he'd heard about. They took a table on the patio. It was September but very warm out. She let him order. Arman had died in the early '90s. He was a professor of French at the university by then and his death had been noted briefly in the culture section of *DN*. One of his books about French cognates had caused a minor controversy. She remembered it well. His obituary mentioned two children, a daughter and a son. Maybe one of them had moved into her building.

"News from home," she said after the waitress had brought their drinks, water for Jonas, white wine for Louise. Jonas hadn't lived with Louise and Martin for more than a decade, but she still thought of the apartment as his home. "The apartment across the courtyard finally sold."

"The neighbor who died?" he said. "Dad mentioned it." Martin served on the co-op board and would have known about the sale. He rarely shared such information with Louise.

"That's right," she said. "Barbro Ekman. Her children had been trying to sell the place for months. You can't imagine the smell when the body was first discovered." The apartment, which was one floor lower than her and Martin's, had been empty since Barbro Ekman died before Christmas the previous year. Her body was found only after Martin, who'd been up in the attic storage area on that side of the building to retrieve a box of decorations, smelled the decomposition. The air was sour and rotten, even two floors up. He'd been upset,

Louise remembered, that no one in the building had noticed for so long, that no one who lived closer to Barbro Ekman had been alarmed by the overwhelming stench of her rotting body. "They're all so selfish," he'd said. But Louise suspected he was really only upset that he'd been the one to make the discovery.

Jonas took a drink of his water. "Gruesome," he said.

It had been snowing the day the cleaning company came. She watched from her kitchen as they worked. They scrubbed walls and floors, removed furniture. They even took some of the fixtures and appliances from the kitchen. The idea that humans are so unclean on the inside preoccupied Louise for weeks. "Well," she told her son, "I can't imagine what a relief it must be to her family."

"I don't think I ever met that woman," said Jonas. "Not that I remember."

"She was very old," Louise said. She couldn't tell if he was telling the truth or only saying this to annoy her.

From the bedroom on the courtyard side of their apartment, there was a clear view of Barbro Ekman's living room. When Jonas was young, that bedroom had been his. Now Martin used it as an office. She rarely went in the room anymore. Martin was private about so much. "Do you remember the blue light from her window?" she asked Jonas. "How it used to reflect on the flower box?"

"I think so," he said.

"It used to scare you."

He tore open the paper wrapping of the chopsticks, pulled them apart, and rubbed them together to smooth the edges.

"It was so easy to explain," she said. "It's just her television, I always told you. But you never believed me."

The waitress arrived with two rectangular plates and set them down in the center of the table. Colorful pieces of fish were arranged on each plate. She'd tried to listen to what Jonas had ordered and follow along in her own menu, and she'd easily been able to do so, but now that the food had arrived she couldn't tell one piece of fish from another.

Jonas pointed with his chopsticks. "Salmon," he said. "And yellowtail. Whitefish. Eel on this plate here."

She'd always disliked eel. Eel could travel great distances out of the water and she found this disturbing.

"Who bought the apartment?" Jonas asked.

"I only know a name," Louise said. Arman had been a good teacher. She could still recite the conjugation of several French verbs, hear his voice reading from lists he'd put on the chalkboard. Present indicative, present conditional, present subjunctive. She remembered the strangest things. There couldn't be that many Jahanis in Stockholm. Jonas was thirty-four. Would she feel jealous or relieved if the person in the apartment was close to that age?

She watched her son eat.

He talked about a problem at his office. An e-mail had been accidentally sent to the wrong person and Jonas found this uncomfortably funny. He'd only been in his current position for a year and everything he said about his job, positive or negative, surged with fresh excitement.

When they finished, Jonas insisted on paying the check. As he was figuring out the tip, she typed an e-mail to herself on her phone with a reminder to deposit money in his account.

She walked him back to work. They said good-bye to each other outside the glass-walled entryway of the building's lobby. Jonas vanished into the crowd of office workers. It was remarkable how similar to her son they all looked. It had been the same when he was in school. They were all identical. Hundreds of them crowded the spaces of his childhood. His soccer matches, ski lessons, piano. She'd always been at ease with being the mother of a child who was like everyone else. It had been a relief to exist so close to the middle. She'd believed this all her life. There were so many fewer risks. She watched the crowd fill the lobby. These could all be my children, she thought.

She decided to walk home. Systembolaget had a location near Jonas's office and she wanted to buy a bottle of wine. It embarrassed her to buy wine more than twice a week from the same Systembolaget and she'd been to the location closer to her apartment only the day before. Lately, she'd been interested in South African wines. She picked two bottles of a cabernet that, according to a sign fastened to the shelf in the store, had ranked very highly in a blind taste test. She paid for the wine, and, as she left the store, she looked up and down the street to see if there was anyone who might recognize her. Then she stuffed the bottles into her purse, concealing what wouldn't fit all the way in with her scarf, and walked the rest of the way home.

The green piece of paper was still there on the call box, partly obscuring the name Ekman. One corner of the paper curled outward in the heat. With her fingernail she started to peel the tape up so she could reposition it over the paper but she stopped herself.

The stairwell was dark. Someone in an apartment on the ground floor was playing music very loudly. The volume faded as she climbed the stairs. By the second floor, she could no longer recognize the song.

She set her purse on the kitchen counter. The bottles clinked. Her purse muffled the sound. It was two, according to the oven clock. Martin was at work. That evening he was going out with colleagues to celebrate his retirement. They were taking him to a karaoke bar. She didn't expect him to be home until late. Martin was retiring early. They didn't need the money and he was bored with work. She opened one of the bottles of wine and poured herself a glass. Sometimes she worried she was damaging her health. The music was still playing and it seeped clearly into the kitchen. She took her wine to the balcony and sat looking out over the courtyard. The curtains in Barbro Ekman's apartment were drawn and the apartment was dark. A new song came on, one she recognized. She mouthed along to a few words of the chorus, took a sip of her wine. The wine tasted good and the song reminded her of someplace nice. She couldn't place the memory exactly, but the song made her think of the outdoors, of a beautiful view. There were trees and snow. Maybe the song had been on the radio frequently during a trip they'd once taken. The stairwell light flickered.

In the apartment just below Barbro Ekman's place lived a woman named Johanna. Her two sons were grown now. One of them played ice hockey in America, somewhere in the southern states, Louise thought, North Carolina maybe. The other was a lawyer up north in Kiruna. Louise remembered when the family first moved in. Now the boys were grown, though they'd seemed so young when they first arrived. That was right before Louise had gotten pregnant with Jonas. She liked the family. She'd helped the boys plant a small herb garden on her own balcony because it faced east and got good morning sun.

Once, about a month before Jonas was born, Johanna had asked Louise to come sit with the older of her sons. The younger one was very sick, and Johanna hadn't wanted to take them both to the hospital. Louise wasn't feeling well herself and didn't want to get sick with whatever the boy had. So she volunteered Martin to go in her place.

After barely an hour, he came back. She heard his footsteps in the hall outside their apartment. She heard the front door open and Martin's heavy steps as he walked back to the bedroom. He was tired, he told her, and had forgotten to take a book to read.

"Who's watching him?" she asked. "Has Johanna come back?" The bed was warm and comfortable, and Martin's silhouette in the doorway appeared much larger than he actually was.

"I need to find my book," he said.

"They have books there," she said. "And a television."

"I'm tired, Louise," he said. The shadow of her husband stepped out of the doorway and disappeared into the hall. She heard a door open and close, then another. Then the airy creak of leather as he settled himself down into his chair in the living room.

She got out of bed and wrapped herself in her robe. It had happened many times since, but this was the first time she could remember hating her husband. Over the years that became such a familiar, even comfortable, feeling. It was cold out and she crossed the courtyard as quickly as she could. She was careful to avoid an icy patch where the shadow from a first-floor balcony kept the ground wet even in the warmest part of the day. Before she'd reached the door to the other building, a gust of wind blew and she felt the chill on her bare legs.

She could remember so much about that evening but not what the problem with the boy had been. She couldn't recall Johanna coming home. But she remembered distinctly waking up on Johanna's couch, her throat and stomach on fire with heartburn and hatred for Martin. The next time she saw Johanna, she'd ask about that night. We inhabit memories so differently from one another. Or, better, our individual memories of a shared event mean such different things to each of us. It had something to do with identity, she supposed, but she didn't feel like chasing after the thought any further.

She spent the rest of the afternoon on the balcony or else on the narrow, soft couch in the sitting room, reading. Days passed quickly when she drank. By five o'clock the sun had dipped behind the building to the west and the temperature dropped. Louise had nearly finished the first bottle of wine. When her neighbors started to arrive home after the workday, she went inside and sat at the kitchen island. She was careful about appearances. Sometimes she threw away bottles instead of taking them to the recycling because she didn't want her neighbors to see how much she drank.

She fixed herself something to eat and opened the second bottle of wine. She watched the news while she ate. Dusk settled over the courtyard and by eight it was dark. She shut the television off and took a thin blanket from the couch and returned to the balcony. She wrapped the blanket around her shoulders. Outside the apartment, she could smell her own inside life distinctly on the blanket. The courtyard was dark. She tried to find a pattern in the lit-up windows on the building opposite. Two dark, one light. Three light, one dark, three light. Windows lit up and darkened and she could never get past a third position in the pattern and soon gave up trying and enjoyed the evening. Occasionally, the building's front door would open loudly and slam shut. The hall light switched on and then off with every neighbor who came home or left. She heard voices, a television, laughter. Barbro Ekman's apartment was still dark.

She was the one who'd ended things with Arman. She'd gotten pregnant and the idea that the baby might be his had frightened her. Of course, the timing wasn't quite right. The last time she'd slept with Arman was weeks before the likely conception date. She'd been relieved to understand this when the midwife circled the estimated due date on the colorful chart she held in front of Louise and Martin in the cramped exam room at the thirteen-week checkup. Louise felt as if she'd risked something great and survived. The chances of that happening twice were small. She hadn't told Arman she was pregnant. It was better that he didn't know. Just after the birth, the first time she held Jonas against her chest, she felt the sticky wetness of her own blood on his body, she touched his hair. It was dark, curled wet with blood and amniotic fluid. Until the midwife had washed him and given him back to her, she was terrified that perhaps Jonas was Arman's after all, that she'd miscalculated some crucial fact.

The heavy front door of the building creaked open. The light in the front hall came on. It sparked out into the courtyard, revealing a chair and the sharp contrasts of shadowed corners. The door slammed shut. She listened to footsteps in the stairwell. Her wine glass was empty and she got up to fill it. In the warmth of the apartment, she felt a chill in her feet. She filled her glass and held the bottle up in front of her to check how much wine was left. Just over half.

She took the bottle with her back to the balcony and sat in the darkness. She was warm and didn't need the blanket. The lights in Barbro Ekman's apartment had been turned on. Through the curtains, she saw movement. She watched the windows closely. There were three, spaced evenly from one end of the building to the other. Kitchen, living room, bedroom. There was a bathroom and a small dining room on the other side of the apartment. She knew this because she'd once been inside, years before, to help Barbro Ekman move a painting from the hall to the bedroom. Barbro Ekman had been dead for eight months. She was a young ghost. Louise watched the figure move from window to window, its dark shape heavy in the living room where the light was brightest, faint in the bedroom.

Martin wouldn't be home for hours. He never came home when he said he was going to. She couldn't remember how Arman Jahani had died. Probably some disease. Most people die in unassuming ways like that. Quiet but painful struggles consisting of medicines and doctor visits, hope established, quickly abandoned. It was so boring. Better to die like Barbro Ekman had. By the time Jonas was very young, two or three perhaps, she'd nearly forgotten that she had once thought he might be Arman's son. She couldn't remember what it had been like to feel any guilt about it. The wine was good, but it had left a sticky film in her mouth and she didn't want the rest. She got up to find something else to drink.

In the kitchen, she poured herself a glass of scotch from the bottle that Martin saved for special occasions and guests. She didn't like scotch, particularly, but this tasted good. It stung her throat. She coughed, took another sip. What would it have been like to raise Arman's son? Without imaging any details she felt the idea forming, shapely and full, and was able to hold it firmly in her mind for just a moment. What did it matter? Arman was dead. That was the simplest truth of all. Would Martin have figured it out? He'd been a good father, a little distant, a little too rooted in his work, perhaps, but that was normal. Jonas had had a good childhood. She was happy she hadn't had to carry a lie as big as his life with her all this time.

She emptied her glass, winced, searched the burn of the scotch in her throat for pleasure. On the balcony she filled the empty glass with the rest of the wine and sat in her chair and drank. In Barbro Ekman's apartment, Arman's real child was alive. It was funny how her path and Arman's, such a ridiculous metaphor, had converged. He would have found it amusing. She was sure of it.

The figure came to the window in the kitchen, pulled the curtains to one side, and opened the window. Arman had a daughter. Louise watched her sit at the table, the light from the lamp forming a bright circle at the center of the table. She was drinking something from a mug. Coffee or tea, maybe wine, Louise thought.

She and Martin had lived in the building longer than everyone but grouchy old Jan Lindblom down on the ground floor and Barbro Ekman, of course, before she'd died. Back in the kitchen, Louise poured another finger of whiskey. It tasted a little like wine but it wasn't bad. In the cupboard, she found an unopened package of cookies. Shortbread, the kind Martin liked.

The stairwell was dark. She took the first steps carefully, her hand against the smooth wall as a guide. As she descended, the light from the courtyard brightened and eventually she could walk without fear of falling. Outside, she looked up at her balcony. The light from her kitchen was inviting, soft orange and yellow. Warm colors. She would never do this sober.

The name was on the mail slot on the door. Jahani. She knocked. Footsteps. The young woman answered. She was beautiful, as far from the middle as Louise's son was near it. "Hello," the young woman said.

"I live here," said Louise.

"I'm sorry?" the young woman said.

"I meant I live in this building and I wanted to welcome you."

"That's very nice," the young woman said. "Thank you so much." She looked back into the apartment. Louise peered in too. There were open boxes, a leaning stack of blankets and towels, an empty bookcase turned at a funny angle at the end of the hall. "I was unpacking." She smiled. Louise could tell she was embarrassed.

Louise smiled back and didn't move. "You've just moved in," she said.

"Officially tomorrow," the young woman said. "Getting a head start. Sara," she said and held out her hand.

Louise took it. "Louise," she said. It was difficult to re-call exactly what Arman had looked like. She might have seen him in Sara. But had he been tall? Sara was tall, taller than Louise. He had dark hair and she remembered him as very thin, but also strong. *Sinewy* was the word for it. He had thick veins on his arms. "I live just over there," she said. She held the box of cookies out to indicate the direction of her apartment.

Sara looked at her.

"Oh, listen to me," Louise said, handing the cookies to Sara. "These are for you. Welcome."

"You didn't have to do that," Sara said.

"Of course," said Louise. "I wanted to. You're one of us now."

Sara smiled.

Louise's face and the top of her chest were warm. She touched her fingertips to her throat. "You'll like living here," she said.

"I think so too," said Sara.

Louise didn't believe in fate. Every morning she woke up with the thought that that day would be the one something terrible was destined to happen. She did this because she didn't believe it was possible to predict the future, to know what was coming for each of us. Whatever she believed would happen that day she knew could not, by nature of our inability to predict the future. Lately, she'd been imagining terrible things. Car accidents, robberies, disease. Martin thought it was unhealthy and told her so frequently. "This is a good area," she said. "We've been here for years. It's very safe."

Sara fidgeted at the door. "I like this neighborhood. I always have." She held the cookies in front of her, took a step back into her apartment, smiled politely, and put her hand on the door.

"You could be my daughter," Louise said.

"Excuse me?" Sara said. She let her hand fall from the door.

"I could have been your mother. I knew your father before you were born."

Sara squinted a little bit, turned her head slightly to the left. "You've mistaken me for someone else."

"Your father and I were friends," said Louise. "We had a relationship."

"I think you've mistaken me for someone."

Louise reached out and touched Sara's arm. "It was a long time ago. I was in love with him."

Sara smiled and in the smile Louise, even drunk, located judgment. This was how Jonas looked at her, Martin too. The same sad eyes, the narrow, thin-lipped smile. They pitied her, thought she was ridiculous, incapable, unwell. She hated them all. "A woman died here," she said.

Sara started to push the door closed. "Thank you again," she said. "I really should get back to unpacking."

"She was very old, the woman who lived here before you," Louise said, stepping forward until she'd nearly entered the apartment. "Her body was found just before Christmas last year. I think she had a stroke."

"I'm sorry," Sara said.

"I thought you should know," Louise said. "I'd want to know." She put her hand on the door.

Sara looked at her and Louise saw the pity again. "Are you feeling all right?" Sara said.

"Her name was Barbro," Louise said. She closed her eyes "The woman who used to live here. She was very old. I think that's the best way to go, don't you? In your sleep, just like that. I don't want to sit around waiting for it."

"Can I help you get back home?" Sara said. "Do you think you'll make it on your own?"

"They've cleaned your apartment. You can't imagine the smell. Martin told me about it."

"Do you need help walking back?"

Louise concentrated on holding her head as still as possible. "No," she said. "It's just over there."

In the courtyard, she looked up at Barbro Ekman's apartment. The blinds were drawn. The light in the front room had been turned out. She was cold. She turned the light on in the stairwell, listened to her shoes click and shuffle against the hard stone. From one of the ground floor apartments loud applause and laughter from a television mocked her. She steadied herself with a hand on the cold wall.

She sat at the kitchen island, on one of the tall stools, the wobbly one, and finished the food she'd fixed earlier. She ate most of a piece of bread with too much butter and drank more scotch. Arman Jahani did not have a daughter. She was sure of this. It was late and she was tired. Martin would be home soon and she wanted to be in bed before he arrived. She stood up to pour herself a glass of milk. Milk soothed her stomach. She would be hungover in the morning but she didn't care. She reached for a glass on the far side of the counter and as she leaned forward she brushed the plate off the counter and to the floor. Shattered fragments of china tickled her bare feet.

The plate was not a plate. It was only dozens of pieces of thick ceramic, the patterned lines and shapes disrupted, taken apart, put back together to form something new. She got down on her knees and moved the largest piece to one side and began to place the smaller pieces on top. The edges were sharp and she held each piece as tenderly as possible.

She knew it was Martin before he even opened the door. And when he entered the room, she didn't need to look up to see that she'd been right. "I've made a mess," she said. She pushed aside the plate and picked up a bit of bread with her fingertips and put the bread in her mouth.

"You don't have to do that," Martin said. "Please. I'll get it later."

"Forgive me."

"I'll help you to bed," Martin said.

"You should have stayed, Martin. You could have stayed. It wasn't difficult." She felt his hand on her head. He probably didn't know the night she was talking about but that didn't matter. She leaned forward, devoted, rapidly filling her mouth with the bread as if she were kneeling at the altar of a darkened church.

The Winter War II

A large frowning sun rushed from one side of the screen to the other. Then the bald-headed meteorologist with the ponytail called for snow on Easter Day. He heard the door open, heard the echo of the stone-floored hallway, and there was a man in the room with him. The man kissed Bent on the cheek, and the channel went to commercial. It was a familiar one. Big discounts if it snowed on Easter. A storm was coming. The man said something. Bent heard, answered on instinct. "I suppose it is," he said. "One has to take risks now and again."

It was Bent's birthday. Eighty-eighth, he thought, maybe eighty-ninth. What did it matter? The war was coming. "There's a war," he said. One minute he'd forget this, the next it'd be there, pressing as hard as ice trapped in a narrow bay.

The man held a bouquet of pink and yellow up at his face, smiled behind it. "A vase," Bent heard. The man went to the kitchen. Bent heard kitchen sounds. Water running, a refrigerator door suctioning closed, a cupboard slammed shut. Then a man came out of the kitchen. He looked familiar but Bent couldn't place him. "Who are you again?"

The man laughed. "Your grandson. Lennart. I'm here to take you to the museum. *The Winter War,* remember?" Snow fell onto the balcony. A rusty old chair buried.

Lennart was talking, standing up, moving lips. Bent caught little of it.

The war pressed at his skull, pressed him toward a memory. Had it already been or was it on its way?

"You should wear a suit tonight," Lennart said.

"Where am I going?" Bent asked.

"The film," said Lennart. *"The Winter War."*

Small details stuck. Morning, 1939, winter. The Soviets had invaded Finland. Article in the paper about bombings, Mannerheim. Three neighbors had already gone off to fight, one a flight mechanic, two in a ski unit. Bent was in Humlegården Park, trying to decide if he should go fight too. There was a need. Swedish volunteers were being accepted. Bare trees lined the pathway. A circle of stone benches surrounded a statue of Carl Linnaeus. The first flakes of snow fell atop orderly hedges.

The palms of Lennart's hands brushed roughly down Bent's shoulders, pulling him from that park, from that snow to another. The balcony railing outside had transformed to white. "It's been a long time since you've worn this?" Lennart asked.

"I don't remember," Bent said.

In the taxi on the way to the museum, Lennart spoke.

Bent listened to the tires on the icy road. Slush from the salt and vehicles. A bus skidded to a stop at a station.

The museum was all bright lights and white smiles and crowds of noisy people. They floated by all of it, stopped among rows of chairs facing a wall of thick curtains. The room was humid and sticky. They took seats near the front. The curtains parted. On the screen appeared the image of a summer cottage, white trim, iron-red walls, and a small garden surrounded by a short, white fence.

A man walked in front of the screen and tapped his chest. Static, booming voice. "Welcome to *The Winter War*," the voice said, and the man disappeared from the stage.

Light, slow, exposed shaking bare branches of two tall birches to the left of the cottage. Dark, then light. Night, then day. A single flower, red, in the garden bloomed. Others soon followed. Bent knew what he was seeing. This was time, sped up. Or else all else was slowed. Leaves fell to the ground. It rained. The rain turned to snow. Snow covered the grass, the roof. The garden was buried in white. The cottage was the shape of a cottage only clumsier. Icicles reached for the ground from the rain gutters. A gray sky pinned it all down.

In the winter he saw them. A group of soldiers crouched in a trench, dressed in white capes that blurred the falling snow against the dirt. Some of the soldiers stood and looked over the edge of the trench at the cottage and the violent storm engulfing it. Rifles leaned against the dirt. Bent shook at the sound of an approaching plane. Gunfire, shouting. Bombs whistled down, explosions filled the room. The room lit up orange. Snow and dirt rained down on the soldiers, who all crouched low and covered their heads. There was smoke. The clumsy little cottage stood still in the smoke.

Clouds parted and the snow stopped. Bright sun re-flected off shrinking mounds of snow. Bent looked down and removed the hood of the white cape of the dead man beside him, dead face looking up at the sky. He knew this man. If not this man then another. They were all the same, dead soldiers.

And then it was done. The war was over. The cottage, iron-red again, the fence white and sharp-lined. Grass and flowers grew. Birds arrived. Branches sagged under the weight of new leaves. Bent sat in his chair. His legs burned and his feet felt heavy.

It was Linnaeus that did it. Back in that park. Snowy morning, 1939. A statue of Linnaeus, for his ideas of an orderly world. Bent knew what he needed to do, where he fit, how his life must be classified. At the Finnish Legation, where the volunteers were being commissioned, Bent signed papers that same afternoon.

He let his grandson lead him by the elbow to the bar where he was given a beer and placed in another chair. He watched his grandson drink two drinks, then a third. The boy squirmed in his chair, twice tried to say something Bent didn't hear. Single words arrived from Lennart's chair, his face leaned close to Bent. *Film,* he heard. *Marie, apartment.* He couldn't make sense of it so he just watched Lennart twist and turn, cross his legs, uncross his legs, another gulp from a glass. His son Rolf, who was dead, had had the same unending flow of nervous movement. Bent watched his grandson, looked at his son. Time guttered. Rolf was alive and then he was not. The unsteady flame of the memory.

Lennart, somber-faced, stood eventually. Bent allowed himself to be led to the taxi stand. A whistle sounded, arms waved, tires crunched over packed snow and salted gravel.

They drove home slowly in the snow. The snow fell thick, heavy with water, onto the windshield. The driver gripped the wheel hard, stuck his head close to the glass, fogging two round circles with the breath from his nostrils.

Soon they were home. And Lennart was before him, kneeled, pulling off first one shoe then the other, lifting one socked foot to free the cuff of Bent's pants, and Bent stood nearly naked, his body one he still did not recognize below him. Himself, his son, his grandson, these unfamiliar bodies.

In bed, he listened to the murmur of the television from the other room. Explosions or laughter. First of February 1940, Bent arrived with a group of five thousand volunteers at Märkäjärvi to relieve the Finnish battalions fighting there. The winter had been harsh, and supply lines from the bases at Boden and Tornio were disrupted regularly. Deep drifts of snow skulked high up the pines. All along the line, trenches and encampments yawned from the frozen earth. He was ordered to a position just north of the line. Through a thick stand of pine to the south, smoke from a Russian fire reached across the gray sky. It was nearing dark. Only midday, but the clouds were so thick the light remained unchanged for the hours he crouched in the trench, rifle trained on the smoke and flicker of movement through the trees. A head, shoulders, rising embers from a stoked fire. First the cold burned but then it numbed. It circled him in bed now. He had never seen so much snow. The first shots stabbed the dirt. Then mortar rounds, more gunfire. Blood an icy continent at the root of what was left of the man beside him. Outside, a fist of clear sky began to open and the storm cleared, snow in the orange light of the courtyard lighter and lighter until it was gone.

Sweet Water

Marie took her daughter to swim at the beach. They splashed around near the shore. Tove emptied the bag of sand toys, looked disappointed to find only a small bucket and a half dozen filthy plastic molds. There was a shell, a crab, a sea star, some animals Marie didn't recognize. While Tove was occupied with these things, Marie waded out in the water. The cool water gripped her legs. Tove filled the bucket with wet sand, dumped it out, filled it again. She made a messy pile of shells and sea stars. Marie walked backward, watching her daughter, until the water was up to her waist, then her shoulders, and finally deep enough for her to be unable to stand. She floated in the water for a little while. Then she swam back and dried beside Tove in the hot sun.

There was a floating pier just up the beach. Tove had

pointed to the children jumping from the pier into the water when she and Marie walked down to the beach from the metro station. She'd said she'd wanted to try. "You're too young, Tove," Marie had said. "You don't swim well enough yet."

Now sand covered, pink from sunburn on her cheeks and neck, she asked again. "Please," Tove said.

Marie said, "One time, and then we'll go home. Lennart's sister is coming to dinner. I'll need your help to cook." She combed a sweaty clump of Tove's hair back from the girl's sandy forehead.

Tove helped rinse the sand toys in the water. She hummed a song Marie couldn't place. Perhaps Tove had made it up. Marie often worried about the person Tove would one day become. Together they walked along the beach toward the pier.

The pier was wobbly and Tove stopped once they'd stepped on it to look up at Marie. Marie smiled. "It's okay," she said. "Take my hand."

At the edge, they stood and looked down into the dark green water. This far inland the saltwater mixed with the fresh and didn't smell brackish like it did nearer the coast.

"I don't want to," Tove said.

"Shall we go home then?" Marie asked, turning back toward the shore and holding her hand out. She tried not to be frustrated, but she couldn't take her mind off the list of preparations she had before dinner.

"I want to do it," Tove said. "No, I want to jump."

Marie turned back to the water. A cold wind whipped drops of water from her legs. "On three," Marie said. At three, she stopped. Tove's toes curled over the edge of the pier. A cloud passed in front of the sun, and the hair on Marie's arms stood up. Children jumped from either side. Water splashed her and Tove's feet.

A young boy walked up behind them. He touched Marie's back with cold fingertips. Her bathing suit was nearly dry and the coldness of his touch on the small of her back, too adult, too intimate, made her flinch. He stood still, smiling at Marie. She said, "Hello there." It was clear to Marie that he had some kind of disability. His eyes were set wide and his nose was flat against a broad face.

"Maybe she'd be brave if I jumped too?" the boy said.

Marie looked around for a parent or a guardian of some sort. What if he couldn't swim, she thought. Two children in the water would be a challenge and there wasn't a lifeguard that day. No one on the beach was looking at them. The boy's smile hadn't changed at all. He continued to look at Marie and said, as if he'd anticipated her concern, "I'm a very good swimmer. It's not hard and I like it."

"What do you think, Tove?" Marie said. "Should we let this boy teach us how to be brave and strong?" Brave and strong, a term she'd picked up from one of Tove's cartoons or maybe a book. So childish and silly. She'd never thought to criticize such an expression before and was both sad and hopeful about what that meant. Tove would start school in the fall.

Tove turned and lined up at the edge of the pier. She seemed ready to jump and Marie didn't want to do anything that might change her mind, so she took her hand and turned back to the boy. "Ready?" she asked.

The boy reached out and took Marie's hand, which she hadn't expected him to do. She was in between the two children. Their hands were cold and Marie could feel the ridged pruning of their fingertips. "On three," she said, holding their hands tight to her hips.

Before they jumped, Tove pulled her hand from Marie's hand. The boy tilted forward a half step, righted himself. "Careful," Marie said to him. Then to Tove, she said, "Aren't you ready?"

"This time," Tove said. But again when Marie started to count, Tove pulled her hand away. Marie knelt on the pier. The water was dark in the shadow of the cloud. She had a pork loin marinating in the refrigerator but the rest of the meal would take time. Asparagus, potatoes, the smoked salmon rolls that Lennart liked as an appetizer. The apartment was a mess, and Lennart always took too long with the cocktails, serving a second round of drinks when he should be putting the meat on the grill. "Please, Tove," she said. "We're going to be late. Let's jump this time." Mostly it was Lennart's sister, Matilda, about whom Marie was worried. She was younger than Lennart but Lennart was a little intimidated by her, a little scared to disappoint her, let her witness even the slightest social or personal failure. And he often took this out on Marie, getting angry if a meal was served too late or the apartment was unkempt and messy. This frustrated Marie. She disliked being late for anything when Matilda was involved. Matilda always had something to say about parenting, particularly how hard it was to keep to a strict schedule with kids, but how important. Matilda had two children and Marie had never known her to be late or unprepared for anything.

She stood and turned to the boy. "Are you ready?" She tried to sound cheerful but could sense her frustration with Tove growing in her voice. The boy didn't say anything. He was quietly singing a song Marie remembered from when she was a girl. It was a song about jumping into cold water. She hadn't heard it in years. She tried to recall the words but couldn't get past the first few lines in her head before she gave up and took Tove's hand. The cloud had passed the sun and it was warm again. Even the wind felt a little warmer. Tove pulled her hand away. "Wait," she said.

Marie looked at the boy again. "Tove," she said sharply, "you have to think of someone other than yourself."

In May, just a little over a month ago, she and Tove had moved in with Lennart. He'd inherited his grandfather's apartment. It was big enough for all of them, five bedrooms, a formal dining room that Bent, Lennart's grandfather, had used as a library, by far the biggest place she'd ever lived. There'd been no question that Marie would move in, and mostly she was happy with the change. Lennart was good to them. He was kind, attentive with Tove, and it was good to be in the city, close to her work. The school Tove would go to was only a few blocks from the apartment and much better than the one she would have attended in the suburbs where they used to live. Safer anyway, and that was important.

A small wave, wake from a passing boat, rocked the pier gently. Marie felt her body adjust to keep its balance. She watched Tove do the same. When the pier settled, she took Tove's hand. Tove looked up at her. Very little time had passed since they came out to the pier and met the boy. But Marie felt as though the afternoon was quickly wasting away. It was ridiculous, she knew, and she tried to fight off the feeling by playfully nudging Tove with her hip. "It's not cold at all," she said. "Nothing to be afraid of. Jump in."

The boy released his hand from Marie's. He stood at her side for a moment, likely to see if Tove was going to change her mind and then, when it was obvious that she wasn't, took off running back down the pier to the beach. "Shouldn't we go, too, Tove?" Marie asked.

Tove took a step and Marie felt her daughter's weight shift, a subtle rising of the pier. But Tove didn't jump. Marie pulled at Tove's hand and Tove looked up, scared. "No more," Marie snapped. "We're going home now."

Tove cried the entire walk back to the metro station and kept crying while they waited for their train to arrive. She dutifully followed Marie onto the train, taking a seat across from her in a cramped foursome of dirtied fabric seats, still crying. Marie got one or two sympathetic looks from other passengers. An old man tried to get Tove to laugh by making faces at her but Tove just stared at the man and kept crying. Eventually, the man gave up and got up from his seat at the Alvik station without saying anything. The ride into the city took about thirty minutes and by the time they'd reached their stop, Tove had stopped crying and was recounting for the second or third time that day something funny that happened at her preschool.

At home, Marie fixed dinner and did the dishes and made coffee and put Tove, who appeared to have forgotten the incident at the pier and was happy and giddy with exhaustion, to bed. Marie didn't bristle once at any of Matilda's comments at dinner or afterward. She smiled at them, in fact, agreed even, imagining that the comments were not directed at her but rather meant in confidence, in solidarity, one accomplished parent to another. Later that night when she and Lennart were in bed and Lennart moved close to her and clumsily pushed his fingers beneath the waistband of her pajama pants, she didn't stop him even though she was tired and the coffee she had had after dinner upset her stomach and she knew he would take too long because of all the wine he'd drunk. When finally he had finished and was asleep beside her, she lay tucked warmly under the blanket until it was clear she wasn't going to get to sleep. She got up, careful not to wake him.

A book that Lennart had read with Tove earlier was on the small antique hall table outside Tove's bedroom door. Without thinking, Marie picked it up. The book was *Comet in Moominland* by Tove Jansson. Tove was named after the author. Pirjo, the Finnish woman who taught the Lamaze course Marie had taken, gave the book to Marie. An early birthday gift, she called it. It seemed like a lifetime ago. The book had always been one of Tove's favorites.

Marie fixed herself a cup of tea and sat at the kitchen table. She was reading a novel, a Danish crime novel that was big and unfocused, and she thought about getting it from the bedroom, but she didn't feel like reading such a book when she was having trouble sleeping. The television would wake Lennart, and anyway she hadn't learned how to use the different controls and settings yet. So many simple parts of her life here were as yet unresolved. She opened *Comet in Moominland,* sipped her tea, which was too hot. She read quickly, trying to enjoy the story. The illustrations were silly but beautiful in a way, too; *otherworldly* was maybe the word for it. She came to the part when Moomintroll discovered that a comet was going to strike the valley and destroy it. He was scared for his family and for his home. Every time they read the book together, Tove would grip Marie's hand at this part, terrified, until her hand released with delight at the end. She hoped Tove would always be capable of surprise, but she knew that wasn't going to be true. It hadn't been true for herself. She flipped to the end and read, longingly, as the Moomin family rejoiced that the comet had passed over them and left their valley safe.

Migration

The Germans were arguing about directions. Lennart understood some German—he'd studied it at school—but he was having a hard time following what they were saying. Beside him on the seat, a dozen bird decoys in a clear plastic bag stared up at him. He sipped his coffee, listened for words he knew. They hadn't left the hotel parking lot yet. He'd met the Germans in the bar the night before, Saturday. The bar was crowded and Lennart had found himself sharing a booth with the Germans. They were biologists, and had already been very drunk by the time Lennart sat down. He couldn't remember the name of the university where they worked, but he remembered that it was near a lake and that they'd come to Denmark to research birds. They were married. He remembered this too. Anneke was a little taller than her husband,

Matthias, and she talked more than he did. Near the end of the night, over shots of Danish bitters, Anneke had insisted Lennart join them in the morning. "The Mile," she'd said and swept her arm out in front of her, nearly toppling a row of empty glasses, "is unlike anything else." He'd tried to decline the invitation but Anneke insisted. "Tomorrow is your last chance," she said. "We leave Sunday." Lennart planned to go home Sunday too. He agreed to join them, assuming that even if he remembered the commitment in the morning he'd be tired or else sleep late and miss them.

At six or so he woke up, still wearing his shirt and his socks, the television whispering to the room. He dug his head under the lumpy pillow. The pillow smelled strongly of detergent and beneath that some musky, human smell. By seven, he was sitting up in bed with a cup of terrible hotel coffee muted by a splash of whiskey. The television, which had been playing an endless loop of short advertisements regarding local attractions, flashed to a sweeping aerial shot of wide dunes, gripped in places by patches of tall grass. Immediately, he understood this must be Råbjerg Mile, where the Germans were going to take him. He felt a swab of drinker's shame pass over him as he remembered the invitation.

It was Marie's idea that he come to Denmark. She had suggested the trip so that he might get away, as she put it, from a rotten year. It was true his year had been challenging. Last June his father had died. Then the following April, about a week before Easter, his grandfather died. Lennart discovered the body, had been the one to let the police and the coroner into the apartment. All of it was sad and exhausting. He had been a difficult person to live with in the last year. For one thing, he drank too much and was moody. He was prone to get angry, or worse, turn inward and shut down, ignore Marie and Tove for long stretches. They'd all moved into Lennart's grandfather's apartment that spring and for the most part the arrangement was working fine. He was happy with Marie. They rarely fought. He enjoyed being around her, talking with her. They made love often enough, and he loved Tove as if she were his own daughter. But beneath all that there was a sense of finality, of permanence, pressing on him. It was immature, he knew, to feel so much anxiety about the ways his life had changed, and continued to change, now that they were a family. It bothered him more than the deaths of his father and grandfather. Marie had convinced him to come to Skagen. She told him about the art galleries and restaurants and the waves that crashed into each other where the North Sea and the Baltic meet. She made the place sound restorative, but to Lennart it was cold and dreary and he'd barely managed to make it out of his room at all.

The trip so far had been a failure. He'd been concocting lies all week about where he'd been and what he'd done. She would be disappointed if she knew the truth. He'd gone so far as to stop outside an art gallery on one of his daily walks to take note of the exhibiting artist's name so that he might tell Marie about the paintings. In truth, he'd mostly spent the week drinking in his room and, in the evenings, at the hotel bar. By Wednesday, he'd achieved a kind of mania that scratched and buzzed at him deeply, so much so that he was incapable of controlling his own decisions and actions. He simply experienced them. So when he got up and packed a small bag to take with him to the dunes, he found that each of his movements was deliberate, inevitable, and he did not stop to question himself. His body acted before his mind. It was out of character for him to agree to such a trip, or any-way out of character to actually follow through with it, but in the context of his behavior in Skagen so far that week, it made perfect sense.

In the mirror, he gave his face a close inspection and de-cided he didn't need to shave. Then he showered and dressed, and met the Germans close to eight in the dining room. There was some awkward small talk as they made their way to the parking lot and more still when Anneke tried to insist he ride in the front seat and Lennart refused, a process that was repeated several times until Anneke gave up, which is how Lennart found himself sitting behind her, beside the bag of bird de-coys, listening to her and Matthias argue in German.

Anneke turned around in her seat and said in English, "We're just figuring out a new way to drive to the dunes. Matthias is being stubborn as usual." She swatted at his shoul-der with her hand.

Matthias smiled. He put the car in gear and eased out of the parking spot. "We're off," he said. Then he said something in German to Anneke and touched her leg tenderly.

Soon the city was behind them and the road opened up to a broad flat stretch of land where farms had been squared out across the sandy ground. The wind hummed somberly over the top of the car.

"I hate this song," Anneke said and switched the radio off. "Lennart, do you know very much about the Mile?"

Before Lennart could answer, Matthias said, "This whole area," and pointed back and forth across the landscape with a finger, "is very windy. The sand comes out of the sea on the west side of the peninsula and moves across the land to the east and back to the sea. The Mile is the largest migrating sand dune in Europe."

"Funny to think about, isn't it?" said Anneke. "Moving ground."

In no time, they were off the main road, following the signs, posted in many different languages, to the parking lot at the dune's edge. There weren't many cars in the lot. Matthias parked near the trailhead. Along the ridge of the nearest dunes grass rattled in the wind.

Lennart helped take the equipment from the car.

"Many species of birds breed here in the spring," Anneke said after they'd gone a little bit down the trail. She was breathing heavily with the weight of the bags she was carrying and the difficulty of walking in the deep sand. "In late autumn they come back on their migration south. We think these groups end up in Africa, maybe Italy. We've been hoping to find tags from other countries on the birds so we'll know for sure. So far only the Netherlands and two from France."

Lennart looked at the bag of decoys. He was surprised by how attentive he'd been to Anneke's explanation. He had assumed he'd simply go with the Germans to the Mile and leave them to work while he walked around, maybe read for a little bit, enjoy what was sure to be one of the only warm days of his trip, certainly one of the only activities he could report to Marie, but the Germans' work captivated him and he wanted to stay to watch. "Do you catch the birds?" he asked her.

"With a net," she said. "You'll see. We want to compare population sizes from this year and five years ago, when we came here last. If we see a decrease we know that there has been habitat destruction. Plovers, that's the type of bird Matthias and I study, are a very common and robust species in the north of Europe. To see a decrease in their numbers would be ecologically discouraging."

The wind was warm and he had to squint against the blowing sand. When they'd reached a spot at the foot of a tall rise, where there was an open space between dunes, Matthias dropped the bags he was carrying and said, "Here."

They worked fast. Anneke stretched a large square of dark green nylon between two articulated poles Matthias had removed from a cylindrical case, unfolded, and driven into the sand about two meters apart. She and Matthias tied guy lines to each pole, pulled the lines tight, and fastened them to stakes anchored in the sand.

Using a length of rope, Matthias measured out a rectangle about the size of a small car. This didn't take him long. Soon he was arranging more articulated poles on each side of the rectangle. He then spread out a net and stretched it to reach the poles.

While Matthias worked, Anneke took the decoys from the bag one by one and fastened a metal spike to the undersides. She held one up to Lennart. "Birds are like us," she said. "They'll always come to where they find others." He'd never thought of himself that way but he supposed the morning had proved that he was.

"What happens when the birds land?" he asked.

"See the poles Matthias is working with?" Anneke said, pointing with a decoy. "The joints are hinged. The birds come in like this." She brought the bird back toward her body. "They land beside these decoys and when the wind conditions are ideal, we pull on the line, the net rises up into the wind, and falls over the birds. It's called a clap net."

"Does it injure the birds?" asked Lennart.

"Rarely," Anneke said. She picked up another decoy, pushed the metal spike firmly into the body, and placed the bird with the others. "We've named each of these wooden birds," she said. "It's funny to think about. This one is Frank. Do you have a family, Lennart?"

"A girlfriend," he said. "She has a daughter." Tove had just started school that fall. She was in kindergarten. Most days, Lennart walked with her the three blocks to her school. It was a part of his day he usually liked.

Anneke tapped the decoy on the sand. "Matthias and I aren't really married. Well, he is. I was once, too."

Lennart wasn't sure he'd heard her correctly. She pushed a metal spike neatly into a decoy. He watched this. "I'm sorry?" he said.

"We've worked together eighteen years this fall," she said without looking up from the birds. "When we travel for our research, we pretend we're married. It started as a joke. I think Matthias was just too afraid to tell me what he wanted." Lennart looked to Matthias, who was tethering the net to the poles forcefully. "The first time, we were in France, close to Dunkirk, in a hotel near the beach, I'll never forget. We don't talk about it during the rest of the year. Only when we're on trips like this one. We stay together in one room, we sleep together." She looked down at one of the decoys. "His wife has no idea. We travel twice every year for our work. Once in the fall and once in the spring. I imagine you think it's terrible."

Lennart leaned back on his heels. His legs stretched uncomfortably. "Not at all." Perhaps she was joking and the punch line was going to be his incorrect reaction. Marie did this to him all the time. She'd tell him a story about work or about Tove and if he wasn't listening closely enough and responded the wrong way, she'd tease him for his inattention, for a faulty moral judgment that would allow him to excuse some terrible thing someone at work had done, or a story on the news. He looked at Matthias again. Any second he expected Anneke to cry out with laughter.

"Do you know," Anneke said in a tone that was unexpectedly quiet. She held the decoy out in front of her. "I used to dislike it. But not anymore. It's like living a make-believe life."

Matthias was squatting beside the net and moved quickly, crab-like, farther down the array to the corner closest to Anneke and Lennart.

"After every trip," she said, "Matthias goes back to his wife and their two sons. The boys are almost grown now."

When Matthias had finished with the net, he walked slowly over to where Anneke and Lennart were kneeling. Each of his steps sent a spray of sand up around his feet. He leaned forward and kissed Anneke on the top of her head. She closed her eyes and bowed into his kiss.

Lennart helped place the decoys at even distances across the space where the net would fall. They settled the birds into the soft sand. Matthias checked the hinged joints, lifting and releasing the array several times. The wind filled the blind. Later, Matthias served coffee from a thermos. "Now we wait," he said as he handed Lennart a cup.

They sat in the shade of the blind for a long time. He watched the shadow change shape. He didn't want to seem rude to the Germans so he insisted, whenever either of them offered, that he was more comfortable on the sand. His back hurt. He wished he had something to drink. The sand was warm and the sun was hot when the wind wasn't blowing. He took two short walks up the dunes but never got so far that he couldn't see the Germans. There weren't many other people out. Given the time of year, this didn't surprise him.

It was almost two o'clock in the afternoon when Lennart returned from one of his walks. Anneke and Matthias were speaking in German to each other. Lennart tried to guess what they might be talking about, but he could never seem to string together enough words to be sure. When they'd stopped talking for a little while, Lennart turned to Matthias and said, "Anneke was telling me about your sons." The wind was blowing hard against the blind.

"Our boys," she said and smiled at Matthias. Lennart looked at her, curious if he'd catch a playful smile, some evidence of a lie. "We have two boys. Matthias, after his father, and the younger one is named Karl. We've been so lucky." She stroked Matthias's arm. "Matthias, the older boy, is at Konstanz, where we teach. He's just started and he wants to be an engineer."

"And Karl?" Lennart said. "What about him?" The sun was warm on his face. He closed his eyes. The father of a boy he'd known in school had had a secret family, a wife and three children in Finland. Something small, a postcard or a bill, maybe a birthday card, had caused the lie to collapse. People in the neighborhood where Lennart grew up still gossiped about it.

"Karl lives in Munich," Anneke said. "He works at a bank. We're very proud of him."

Another hour passed and the birds still hadn't come.

Anneke spent the time solving math puzzles in a torn and creased paperback, chewing on the tip of the pen and nodding her head slowly. Her feet were in Matthias's lap. He was leaning back in his chair, his hat pulled down low over his eyes, one of his hands resting across Anneke's crossed legs. Lennart read the newspaper he'd taken that morning from the hotel. There was a car crash in Frederikshavn. Two Volkswagens, identical in every way except that one was from Denmark and the other from Sweden, had had an accident in a traffic circle near the ferry terminal. No one spoke.

Lennart saw the birds first. A low-slung black cloud shook and pulsed on the horizon. He placed the newspaper in the sand. At first he couldn't tell what he was looking at. The cloud moved as if it were a single body. When one side expanded outward, the opposite side followed, closing any open space. He watched for a moment before it occurred to him that he was looking at a flock of birds. "There," he said, pointing. When he spoke he heard that his voice sounded higher-pitched and unfamiliar.

"Come closer to the blind so that you don't frighten them," Anneke said. Lennart crawled through the sand toward Anneke and knelt beside her. The birds approached and a group split from the flock and landed in the sand all around them. They were taller than the decoys and much more dramatically colored. Some had yellow mixed in with black and gray feathers along their backs, and a long S-shaped line of white along the sides of their heads. The birds shook and stepped in short, rapid movements while Matthias and Anneke whispered to each other, also moving quickly, and before Lennart knew it had happened, Matthias pulled the line and the net rose straight up into the wind. The net paused at the apex of its arc and everything seemed to fall silent and then the wind caught the net and it clapped down violently. The birds not in the net exploded into the air from the sand. He listened to the caught birds trying to flap their wings beneath the net. Soon they stopped struggling and there was no noise, only the net rising and falling with the birds' heavy breathing.

Matthias reached under the net and pulled out the first bird. He spoke softly to it as he lifted it up, held it close to his chest. He turned the bird slowly in his hand and lifted each of its wings. Then he placed a blue plastic tag around the bird's leg and crimped it shut with a pair of pliers. He and Anneke took turns removing a single bird at a time, made note of its tag if it had one, fastened their own tag on the bird's leg, performed what Lennart guessed was a brief medical exam, and then released it. This they did by setting the bird down in the sand and waiting for it to fly away.

It took a long time to make it through all but one of the birds. "Twenty-seven," Anneke said to Matthias, who was approaching the final bird. The bird wasn't moving, and as Matthias got closer, he said something to Anneke that Lennart didn't understand. Lennart watched them both to see how he should react. The bird was pinned beneath the pole, the net twisted and knotted around its neck. "It's dead," Anneke said without touching the bird to confirm that she was right.

Matthias lifted the net and untangled the bird. He held it in both hands, looking down at it for a moment, and walked to a stand of grass and placed the bird behind this. Lennart was surprised at how easy this all seemed, but he didn't know what else he would have expected to happen. "That's all?" he said.

"If this was another species of bird," said Anneke, "or if we knew it was diseased, we would freeze the body to study it later. But plovers are common and this one appears healthy. What this bird will tell us about the plover population of Northern Europe is only that accidents sometimes happen."

"Anyway," said Matthias, "we don't have the proper equipment to freeze the bird."

"Shouldn't we bury it?" asked Lennart.

"No," Anneke said. "An animal will find the bird and eat it. The rest will decompose. If you bury it in the sand, the bird will rot."

"Shall we say a funeral prayer too?" Matthias said, laughing. "Light a candle?"

"Don't listen to him. Unceremonious disposal of a dead body is not necessarily an indication of a lack of respect for these birds, or for nature. Animals die. This is normal in any ecosystem. We die, they die. It's nothing."

Lennart watched the Germans finish their work. They took down the blind and disassembled the net and the poles, neatly packing everything. Lennart helped as he felt he could, but mostly he just watched. He tried not to look at the dead bird.

He helped take equipment back to the car, following a short distance behind Anneke and Matthias, who seemed to have been energized by the success of the net and their work and spoke loudly about a restaurant they wanted to try in Skagen that evening. They were nearly back to the car when Lennart remembered the newspaper. He helped the Germans load the equipment in the trunk and the backseat, and then he went back for the paper.

He walked quickly down the trail, struggling to keep his pace in the sand. Up ahead he saw some birds, gulls maybe, circling above. He reached the place where they'd set up the blind and the net. Some larger birds had landed and were pecking at the plover's carcass. When Lennart got close, the larger birds flew off. Anneke had said this would happen, of course, and he knew enough to know it was natural, but something about the tiny, bloodied body of the bird in the sand bothered him. He kicked some sand at it to cover the body, but this didn't feel right either, so he took the paper and opened it and picked the carcass up and wrapped it in the paper as tightly as he could. He didn't know what to do after this, so he opened his backpack and placed the bird carefully inside.

The Germans were waiting in the car when he got back. When he left the trail for the asphalt of the parking lot, he waved and began to jog, no more quickly than he could have walked probably, toward the car. Matthias put the car in gear and started driving before Lennart was settled. The door slammed with the momentum. He held his backpack on his lap. Anneke, her hand rested on Matthias's shoulder, turned in her seat to look over her own shoulder at Lennart. "Did you find what you were looking for?"

He hadn't said why he was going back. "I left my newspaper," he said.

"What did you think of the Mile, Lennart?" Matthias asked.

The grasses and the waves of sand were pretty, a little boring, unsurprising, maybe. He'd liked watching the Germans work, though he still hadn't decided whether Anneke had been joking about her and Matthias. The joke or whatever it was wasn't particularly funny, but given that he didn't know Anneke at all, it hardly seemed like an honest admission. He'd tried to imagine telling Marie about it, but there wasn't really a way, as far as he could tell, to do so without seeming to betray an intimacy with Anneke that he hadn't had. Marie would be curious about the context for such a story and he knew she'd have the same questions he did about the arrangement, whether it was true or not. "There were fewer people than I'd expected," he said finally.

"We're so far from everything up here," Anneke said. "One might really do anything at all."

On the drive back to the hotel, Matthias and Anneke talked more about the restaurant, which had been recommended to them. They were going to leave before lunch the next day. He looked at Anneke for a sign that she was disappointed about the end of the trip. She'd kept her hand on Matthias's shoulder the whole drive, and when Matthias brought up the return trip, suggesting that they stop for the night in Hamburg on the way home, Anneke dropped her hand to his leg and looked away.

At the hotel, he helped the Germans take the equipment inside. He carried his backpack and a black plastic case about the size of his chest. He hadn't remembered seeing the case at the Mile but assumed the Germans' work required all kinds of equipment that he hadn't seen in just one day spent with them. They gathered everything in the lobby, close to the elevators. Matthias went back to the car for the last of the things. It was late in the afternoon, and the sun, low on the horizon, shone in brightly through the tall windows. A nicely dressed couple came out of the bar and crossed the lobby. They walked slowly and deliberately around the equipment. Lennart heard the woman ask the man in a whisper, "Are they making a film, do you think?" The man looked at Lennart and shrugged. He passed very close and Lennart smelled the alcohol on his breath. The day he'd arrived, he'd bought two bottles of Japanese whiskey in Frederikshavn. The first bottle was already empty. He was looking forward to a drink when he got up to his room. When the couple had gone, Anneke leaned close to Lennart. She smelled like sweat but not unpleasantly so. "I know what you did," she said.

"I'm sorry?" Lennart said. His face got warm and he looked past her.

"I'd only guessed it before," she said. "But I can tell I was right by the way you're acting. You did something with the plover, didn't you?"

"I went back for the newspaper," he said quietly. "Like I told you."

"We can't tell Matthias. I think it's kind of funny, even a little sweet, but he'd be angry. Did you bury it? Is that what took so long?"

"Of course not."

"What then?" she said. "You don't have it with you."

"Of course not," he said again.

Anneke looked at his backpack and up at Lennart. "We know something about each other now," she said.

Matthias came in holding the last of the gear. A bag was slipping from his shoulder.

"We were just talking about dinner," Anneke said. "He isn't going to join us after all."

"It's the last night of your trip. I'm sure you'll want some quiet before you go home to your family."

"Well," Matthias said coolly, "come down for a drink later."

In his room, Lennart placed his backpack on the dresser beneath where the television was mounted to the wall. He poured himself a drink and sat down on the bed with it. He flipped through the television channels, watching short flashes of American sitcoms and Danish news programs and a German documentary film about the plastic garbage patch in the Pacific. Several times larger than Switzerland. The narrator said this repeatedly as if it was a precise measurement of size. Lennart got up to refill his glass. He opened the bag and looked inside. The weather forecast was the first thing he saw. A sun and a cloud a single day apart. He reached in and unwrapped the paper and lifted the bird's carcass from the bag. He placed it on the dresser beside his drink. The bird had stiffened a little bit and the beak was tucked tightly against the body. He lifted the bird and looked at the feathers, stretched each wing out to see how long they were. He turned the body in his hands, mimicking as best he could the movements Matthias and Anneke had performed earlier. The bird wasn't tagged. He guessed this meant it was probably young, hadn't had the time to get caught. He put it down and picked up his glass. The glass was nearly empty and this shocked him, though the feeling passed quickly and left a tingle in his chest as if he'd thought he'd lost his car keys or telephone and suddenly remembered they were only in his pocket. The body is so much more immediate to all we experience than the mind. He lifted the glass, held it at eye level, watched the liquid calm, and measured with disappointment how much he'd already had. He finished what was left in one gulp.

Early the morning after his father died he'd received a phone call from the summerhouse. The police had called the evening before to confirm the death, so he was surprised and a little frightened to see his father's number flash across the screen of his phone early the next morning. The call was from

Henrik Brandt, the man who owned the house up the road
and nearest a little outcropping of rock his father had always
called Bull's Head. Henrik had woken him with the call. It
was before dawn. He didn't want anything and he didn't say
why he was in the house. He just apologized for calling so
early and told Lennart he was sorry to have heard the news.
Lennart didn't know how to respond, so he thanked the
man for his concern. It wasn't until later that it occurred to
him that this situation was strange. That afternoon, Lennart
looked up the number for the Uppland County Police Authority and called to report Henrik's phone call. He was
transferred to a woman who introduced herself as a case officer in the Norrtälje Police Department. She assured him that
the police would investigate the call but that it was nothing
he should be concerned about. When he pressed her on this,
insisting he didn't suspect that Henrik was involved in the
death, only that it seemed odd that he would enter the house
of a person he knew was dead and then call that person's son,
the woman said, "People sometimes act in unusual ways following a death." After he hung up, he tried to rest the telephone in its cradle but was distracted and his hand slipped and
he dropped the telephone to the floor, where it broke apart. He
spent that afternoon resoldering a wire to the microphone and
gluing the plastic casing back together as best he could. Then
he called himself from his cell phone several times to check
that the microphone on the landline worked.

   The nature program had ended and the bird was staring
at him. He tried to sip his whiskey, but the glass was empty.
He got up and filled it. The bottle was nearly half gone. He
looked at his reflection in the small circular mirror beside
the television. He hated this hotel. He leaned in and looked

closely in the mirror. Even in the dim shaky light from the television, he could tell his eyes had reddened. He had to do something with the bird.

He wrapped it in the newspaper again, sun and clouds facing him. Tomorrow would be more rain. He held the package in one hand. The drink in his other. He was warm in his chest and the bird weighed nothing at all. He could barely feel it.

With the hand that was holding the bird, he opened the door, pulling until it was wide enough to fit his foot in the crack of light and pull open.

The hall was empty. He held the bird close to his chest.

Next to the elevator was a shiny brass trash can with a large plastic bowl on top that had once been an ashtray. He would put the bird inside, go back to his room, pour himself another drink, watch television until he fell asleep.

Before he could, the elevator bell sounded. He heard the car coming to a stop. The doors opened. Three people stepped out, a man and a woman and a young girl. A family. The woman took the girl's hand and pulled her close, out of Lennart's way, as they passed. "Excuse us," the woman said. She said this in Danish, but Lennart could hear right away she was Swedish. He and Marie had talked about taking a family vacation, but it hadn't happened yet. Maybe in the summer they would take the ferry to Åland to go camping. Lennart felt the bird and his drink in his hand, and turned to hide both from the family. He smiled at them, got on the elevator, and pressed the button for the lobby.

He left his empty glass on the floor of the elevator.

In the dark under the lip of the bar, one hand rested heavily over its tiny shape, he held the bird on his lap. He ordered a beer and drank it quickly. There was a soccer match on television and a crowd of people there to watch. He kept one hand on the bird. With the other he scrolled through his phone, aimlessly. He hadn't checked his e-mail all week. Marie had written to say she was going to meet him at the train station in Stockholm when he arrived on Sunday. She missed him and hoped that his trip had been calming. He wrote back, briefly, to tell her he planned to drive himself to the ferry in Frederikshavn, get the train in Gothenburg, and be home before Tove went to bed. It was simple. He hoped whatever choice he made in the morning was just what he told Marie he'd do, or at least something like it.

It was late when the Germans arrived. The game was over. Lennart still sat at the bar, the bird on his lap, his hand on the bird. Anneke's cheeks were flushed and Matthias was grinning widely. They approached Lennart, sat on either side of him. Matthias put his hand on Lennart's shoulder and squeezed. "What a surprise," Anneke said. "A wonderful dinner, and now this. Now you. Here you are."

Thanks to Anna Stein, and to Ethan Nosowsky, Fiona McCrae, Katie Dublinski, Erin Kottke, and the rest of Graywolf. Thanks also to John McElwee, Alex Hoyt, and Mary Marge Locker, Steve Yarbrough, Ron Carlson, Jill McCorkle, Sabina Murray, Noy Holland, Chris Bachelder, Jack Livings, and Molly Antopol. Thanks to the editors who first published some of these stories, especially Valerie Vogrin, Drew Burk, Maile Chapman, Cal Morgan, Clara Sankey, Brigid Hughes, Lorin Stein, Cressida Leyshon, and Deborah Treisman.

As ever, thanks to my parents and family for their support. And to Anna, with love: thank you.

JENSEN BEACH is the author of the story collection *For Out of the Heart Proceed.* His work has appeared in *A Public Space,* the *New Yorker, Ninth Letter,* the *Paris Review, Tin House,* and elsewhere. He teaches in the BFA program at Johnson State College and lives in Vermont with his family.

The text of *Swallowed by the Cold* is set in Adobe Garamond. Book design by Rachel Holscher. Composition by Bookmobile Design and Publishing Services, Minneapolis, Minnesota. Manufactured by Versa Press on acid-free, 30 percent post-consumer wastepaper.